Part Of Her Still Cringed...

whenever she thought of the uninhibited way she'd responded to his kisses, like some teenager with hyperactive hormones. At the same time, she had to admit he intrigued her. And attracted her. And *dis*tracted her when she should have been concentrating on work.

Even her ex-fiancé hadn't generated such a welter of conflicting emotions. After she'd given him back his ring, she'd vowed not to get involved with another man until she had achieved her self-imposed goals.

Every instinct told her Dan could complicate her life. He was too smooth, too forceful, too damn attractive. And a tiny voice far back in her mind warned her that she was about to take a very dangerous step....

Dear Reader:

Welcome to Silhouette Desire — provocative, compelling, contemporary love stories written by and for today's woman. These are stories to treasure.

Each and every Silhouette Desire is a wonderful romance in which the emotional and the sensual go hand in hand. When you open a Desire, you enter a whole new world — a world that has, naturally, a perfect hero just waiting to whisk you away! A Silhouette Desire can be light-hearted or serious, but it will always be satisfying.

We hope you enjoy this Desire today — and will go on to enjoy many more.

Please write to us:

Jane Nicholls
Silhouette Books
PO Box 236
Thornton Road
Croydon
Surrey
CR9 3RU

Dreams and Schemes

MERLINE LOVELACE

*First published in Great Britain in 1995
by Silhouette Books, Eton House, 18-24 Paradise Road,
Richmond, Surrey TW9 1SR*

© Merline Lovelace 1994

*Silhouette, Silhouette Desire and Colophon are
Trade Marks of Harlequin Enterprises B.V.*

ISBN 0 373 59397 X

22-9501

Made and printed in Great Britain

MERLINE LOVELACE

As a career air force officer, Merline Lovelace served tours of duty in Vietnam, at the Pentagon and at bases all over the world. During her years in uniform she met and married the world's sexiest captain, who subsequently became the world's sexiest colonel, and she stored up enough adventures to keep her fingers flying over the keyboard for years to come. When not glued to the word processor, Merline goes antiquing with her husband, Al, or chases little white balls around the fairways.

One

Naked, wet and shivering, Kate stood framed in the open sliding glass door. Cool night air whispered against her bare back and combined with tentacles of fear to send goose bumps shimmering down her spine. For a long—seemingly endless—moment, she hovered there, one foot over the sill, the other just touching the wood deck behind her. Her eyes narrowed, trying to pierce the dim shadows of the bedroom. Her ears strained to catch an echo of the faint sounds that had made her halt so abruptly.

Another breeze hit her damp skin, causing Kate to clutch her towel tighter. The thin cotton barely covered her front from chest to hip, leaving the rest of her long body exposed to the cool New Mexico night air. She shivered again and tilted her head to one side, listening intently. The only sound she could hear over the pounding of her own heart was the hot tub bubbling on the deck behind her. When no other noise disturbed the summer night, she began to feel a little foolish standing there on one foot, like a tall, goose-pimply stork.

Taking a deep breath, Kate stepped into the dim bedroom and reached for the wall switch beside the door. Soft, warm light bathed the spacious room. Her gaze roamed the undisturbed serenity of a bed and accessories done in muted desert jewel tones of mauve and turquoise. She curled her bare toes into the thick carpet and felt her body relax with the familiar, luxurious sensation.

"You've been reading too many thrillers, Katey m'girl!" she told herself with a slow breath of relief.

Crossing the spacious bedroom, she headed for the wide, raised dais that formed the bathroom. A quick flip of a switch flooded the bath and dressing areas with cheerful light from the overhead spots. Depositing her wet towel in the wicker hamper, she pulled a fresh one from the basket beside the oval tub and attacked her goose bumps. The last of her tension faded with the warmth and light.

Tingling from the brisk rubdown, Kate slipped into a silk sleep shirt. A quick glance in the mirror confirmed that the hot tub had steamed her hair into a wild mass of auburn curls and melted her makeup to the merest hint of color. She ran a brush through her unruly hair without real expectation of subduing its stubborn resistance to any form of discipline. Grabbing a tissue, she wiped the smudged mascara from under her eyes. Her eyes were her best feature, she thought. Wide and clear and a deep violet-blue, they were framed by abundant lashes and a net of fine laugh lines at either corner. At least, Kate told herself that they were laugh lines. At thirty-one, she wasn't ready to admit they could be anything else.

Tossing aside the tissue, Kate wrinkled her nose at her reflection and flipped off the lights. She hummed her favorite tune from *Phantom of the Opera* as she headed for the living room and the work that awaited her. A few steps into the room she stopped, her breath catching in shock.

Her computer no longer sat on her desk. Kate stared at the empty space for a long, confused moment, then turned slowly to survey the large, high-ceilinged room. Stunned, she found a gaping blank space in the bookcase where her miniaturized stereo components once sat. When she saw the doors of the entertainment center hanging open, a frisson of fear darted down her spine. Both the TV and the VCR were gone, as was the collection of hand-carved kachina dolls that had graced the mantel above the adobe fireplace just a half hour ago. Her disbelieving eyes finished their sweep of the living room and fastened on the French doors leading to the enclosed side patio. Sheer, gauzy curtains stirred gently in the breeze beside the open doors.

Tucking her sleep shirt hastily into a pair of jeans, Kate ran to answer the doorbell. She'd called the police only moments ago and gave silent thanks for their swift response. Throwing open the wide front door, she gasped in surprise at the man who stood on the stoop.

He towered over her own five feet seven inches by a good half foot. In the dim porch light Kate made out a square jaw darkened with stubble, a thick, black mustache and eyes that studied her intently. A battered ball cap was perched on the back of his head and a T-shirt with Albuquerque Dukes emblazoned on the front stretched across what seemed like an acre and a half of chest.

Kate didn't take the time to absorb more. She stepped back, arm flexing to slam the heavy door shut.

"Ms. O'Sullivan?"

Her arm faltered in midswing.

"I'm here in response to your call."

The man lifted his hand to eye level, and for the first time Kate noticed the badge in his palm. She peered suspiciously at the metal shield. It appeared genuine, but then she'd never had any dealings with badges or shields before. This man certainly didn't look like any police officer she'd ever seen. Her gaze dropped from the shield to the picture ID right below it. There was no mistaking the shaggy mustache that identified him as Dan Kingman, Albuquerque Police Department.

"Sorry," she told him, stepping back. "I was expecting someone in uniform. Ah, a different uniform."

His lips quirked as he stepped inside. "I apologize for the less-than-professional attire. We were in the middle of our annual charity ball game with the Dukes when I got called out."

"You were pulled out of a ball game to answer my call?" Kate asked, startled. "Isn't that above and beyond the call of duty?"

"Not exactly," Kingman replied, slipping his ID into the back pocket of his jeans. "One of my men wrapped his car around a tree during a high-speed chase in this area. I came to check on him. About the time they cut him out of his vehicle, a rash of reported break-in calls started coming over the net. We have two squad cars in the neighborhood now, taking reports. I was just down the hill when you called, so I decided to take this one myself. Mind if I do a walk-through?''

Kate shook her head and trailed behind him while he searched the house and outdoor areas with quick efficiency.

''Well, it looks like whoever came visiting is gone now. Suppose we sit down and you tell me exactly what happened.''

Kate led the way back to the living room. ''There's not much to tell. I got home from work, spent a half hour or so unwinding in the hot tub and walked in here to find my property missing.''

He pulled a small notepad from his rear pocket, and Kate couldn't help wondering how he managed to fit anything, much less a badge and a notebook in those snug jeans. The glove-soft, skintight material was stretched taut over a pair of muscular thighs. *Very* muscular thighs.

''There were no signs of forced entry. Did you leave any doors unlocked?''

''The French doors were open to let in the air.''

One dark brow arched over hazel eyes. They were an intriguing color, Kate noted, halfway between gray and green, with brown flecks in them. And at this moment those same eyes were regarding her with a faint air of disapproval.

''You mean you just left these living room doors wide open while you went to take a bath?''

''I took a hot tub, not a bath,'' she explained. ''And I always leave the French doors open while I'm home.''

Kingman frowned and glanced around the spacious living room. A blinking light next to the doors caught his attention. ''Was the alarm system activated?''

''No. I don't use it.''

"Why not?"

Kate felt herself stiffen slightly in her chair. She wasn't used to explaining her actions to anyone, especially not to men wearing ball caps with beer logos printed across the bill. She reminded herself that he was a police officer.

"I haven't had time to call the security folks out to rekey it since I rented this place."

"You should," he replied, still frowning. "It would provide some measure of protection for a woman living alone."

His tone was starting to raise her Irish temper. "How do you know I live alone?"

He shrugged. "You don't wear a wedding ring."

"Neither do you," she rejoined. "Does that mean you live alone?"

As soon as the tart words were out of her mouth, Kate regretted them. What did she care about this man's living arrangements?

"Most of the time," he replied solemnly, although amusement danced in his eyes. "Besides, I had a quick look through your bedroom and bathroom. I'm a police investigator, remember?"

"You could've fooled me," Kate muttered to herself.

"Seriously, Ms. O'Sullivan, you should be more careful. Don't fling open your door like you did to me tonight. And get that security system set. A woman your age, living alone, should exercise more caution."

Enough was enough. "Look, Sergeant...ah, Officer, let's leave my age out of this, shall we, and get on with the investigation."

One brow lifted at her crisp tone, then a corner of his disreputable mustache tugged up in a lazy grin. Kate stared, mesmerized by the effect. That the simple rearrangement of a few facial muscles could turn a collection of lean planes and angles into a devastating combination of white teeth, creased cheeks and glinting eyes astounded her.

"Sorry," he murmured. "Didn't mean to touch a nerve."

Kate drew in a deep breath. "No problem. For a moment there, you sounded just like my mother."

Kingman blinked, clearly surprised at being compared to anyone's mother.

"She reminds me on a regular and frequent basis of my age and single status," Kate drawled.

His grin widened. "Let me rephrase that last statement, then. An attractive young woman, living on her own, should take extra precautions. Like setting the alarm system."

"I'll consider it," Kate replied, her chin lifting. Robbery or no robbery, smile or no smile, she didn't like being lectured to.

Kingman studied her for a moment, then gave a slight shrug. "If you'll give me a list of your missing property, I'm done. There's not much to go on, but we'll do our best."

Flipping the notebook shut, the big man got to his feet. "You're sure you didn't see or hear anything?" he asked, moving toward the door.

Kate hesitated, remembering the indistinct sound that had frightened her earlier. "I thought I heard something when I got out of the hot tub. A sort of clicking sound. Nothing identifiable."

Kingman paused, one hand on the front door latch. "Look, I don't want to alarm you, but you live in a pricey neighborhood. It's a natural target. If you won't use the security system, I suggest you keep the French doors closed and locked when you're not in the immediate vicinity.''

"I don't want to be a prisoner in my own home," Kate objected. "The main reason I rented this house was because of its spectacular view."

Kingman let out a long, impatient breath. "I'm not saying you have to barricade yourself inside. Just exercise a little caution. This isn't the first time this neighborhood's been hit. One of my men spoke at a neighborhood meeting last week. I take it you didn't attend?"

"No, Lieutenant . . . um, Detective. I'm only renting this place on a short-term lease. I'll be leaving Albuquerque in three more months. I don't have time to get involved in local issues."

Kingman's eyes narrowed, as if he wanted to say more—a lot more—about her lack of involvement. Kate's chin tilted up another notch.

"You'll have to come down to the police department tomorrow and sign the official report," he said finally. "Ask for Detective Alvarado. He'll be handling the case. I'll give you his name and number."

He pulled a dog-eared card out of a leather case and scribbled across the back. "Here's my card. Call me if you think of anything else. It's 'Captain,' by the way."

Kate closed the door behind him with a mixture of relief and regret. The big man, for all his sexy smile, had rubbed her the wrong way. Still, as she stood in the foyer surveying the living room, she had to admit the house seemed suddenly empty without Kingman's solid presence filling it. Lifting the little card, she studied the bold print. "Captain Dan Kingman. Chief, Criminal Investigations, Albuquerque Police Department."

Card in hand, Kate ambled back into the living room. The soft, muted colors failed to give her the sense of tranquillity they usually did. She wasn't sure whether it was the aftereffects of having her privacy violated or the lingering aura of a certain police officer that disturbed the previously serene room. Whatever it was, she felt restless and edgy.

Tossing the card onto the coffee table, Kate crossed to the French doors to check them once again. Despite her brave words, the robbery had shaken her more than she cared to admit. The thought of someone, or possibly several someones, entering through those doors and invading her home with her in the hot tub, just a few yards away, sent a wave of goose bumps up her arms. She'd worked so hard to reach the point where she could afford some of the luxuries in life. Now she'd had her first taste of the penalties, as well as pleasures, that a beautiful home and fine possessions could bring.

With a determined shrug, she pushed the thought from her mind and headed for her briefcase. Even without her laptop computer, she had plenty of work to keep her busy and her mind off the robbery.

"You mean they came right into your house? While you were there?"

Swallowing a bite of flaky croissant, Kate nodded to the woman sitting opposite her at the small table. "I was in the hot tub. I thought I heard something when I got out, but convinced myself it was just my imagination."

"Jeez, you'd think this was New York or L.A. or something." Tricia Hansen leaned back in the cafeteria chair and held her coffee cup in both hands. "Are you okay? You should have called me last night. Something like that can be pretty traumatic."

"It was, although I have to admit I probably invited trouble by leaving the doors open. As the officer they sent to investigate reminded me, women who live alone—excuse me, women *my age* who live alone!—need to be more careful."

Tricia sputtered into her coffee cup. "I bet you appreciated that!" She toyed with her cup for a moment, then set it down, her expression sobering. "Do you think you should move out of that big house, Kate? You're all alone up there, with no neighbors within yelling distance."

"Oh, no," Kate groaned, "not you, too. I get that same lecture from my mother every time she calls."

"Well, in this instance she may be right."

Kate pushed a hand through her unruly hair. "I love that house, Trish. It's elegant and quiet and has a wonderful view. I was lucky to get it on a six-month lease. And you know I can't take time off to go house-hunting now. With only three more months left on the project, the pace is going to be frantic. Speaking of which," she added, rising, "we need to get back to the lab. I left the two new engineers alone on their consoles."

Trish looked wistfully at the remains of the croissant on Kate's plate and sighed as she pushed back her chair. "I don't know why I even come on these coffee breaks with you. All I do is sip black coffee while you stuff yourself. I wish I had your figure."

"Being so tall does have a few advantages," Kate agreed as the two women strolled down the main corridor of the Phillips Laboratory computer center. "It takes a lot more to fill me up."

"And you don't even pretend to exercise," Trish complained, gesturing toward her own comfortably padded hips.

"I'm constitutionally opposed to strenuous physical activity," Kate declared, punching in the combination to a cipher lock. "Just the *idea* of sweating makes me sweat."

She pushed open a heavy door and passed into another world. Pausing on the threshold, Kate waited for her eyes to adjust to the fluorescent light flooding the vast open bay of the computer center. As her vision cleared, her ears picked up the subdued whir of half a dozen mainframes. A thrill ran up her spine—the same shiver of excitement Kate always felt around computers. There was so much power stored in those neat rows of innocuous-looking machines. Even the new supercomputer, standing by itself at the far end of the huge room, was no bigger than an average-size desk. Yet, that sleek, cream-colored box would be capable of thousands of calculations per second once she got it running.

And that particular box was her responsibility—a fifty-million-dollar machine, and she was the one who'd bring it on-line and integrate it with the lab's other supercomputers. This baby was a far cry from her first computer, a thirdhand one bought during her freshman year at college. She'd had to work extra shifts as a cocktail waitress to pay for that big, now antiquated, machine, but the late hours and lack of sleep had been worth it. Since the first moment she flipped on the power, she'd been hooked.

"All right, team, let's get to it. We've got to get this hummer on-line and start running the first test patterns."

"We're close, boss," one of the new engineers told her, laying the latest spreadsheets out on a wide worktable.

* * *

By the time the last of the crew left that evening, Kate was tired, but euphoric. They'd made more progress than she dared hope. She stuffed scattered papers and thick manuals into a bulging briefcase, grabbed a notebook computer and left the now-silent lab. Using a special access card to exit the front doors of the building, she headed for her car.

Driving the sleek little Audi down the main thoroughfare of Kirtland Air Force Base, Kate felt more cheerful than she had since the shock of the robbery the previous evening. Excitement bubbled in her veins like fine champagne. If her team held to the new schedule they'd worked out this afternoon, they'd finish the project ahead of schedule. That meant she'd be back in L.A. by the end of September with a big, fat bonus.

For the first time since she'd left her job at a high-powered Silicon Valley firm last year and struck out on her own, Kate knew success was within reach. After all those years of paying back student loans, of saving every penny to buy her mother a condominium, of working seven days a week on the toughest projects to gain experience, she was finally on her own and about to make a healthy profit. This was her first big contract as an independent consultant. If she did well, she'd have a secure entrée into the big-money world of supercomputers.

When she got home, Kate was too keyed-up even for the hot tub. She poured herself a celebratory glass of wine and wandered toward the wide doors leading to the patio. Her hand reached for the brass door handle, then hesitated.

With a quick shake of her head, she told herself not to be so timid. Pulling the French doors open, Kate caught her breath at the sight of the high Sandia peaks bathed in the last rays of the summer sun. She settled into an overstuffed rattan chair and watched the mountains turn a deep, glowing pink. Trish, an Albuquerque native, had told her *sandía* meant watermelon in Spanish. Early Spanish colonizers had named this range after witnessing these same spectacular sunsets. Kate sighed and sipped her drink in pure contentment as the pink peaks deepened to red, then to purple. Above them, a velvet-blue sky slowly darkened. Kate felt the quiet beauty of the night wash over her.

"Ouch, dammit!"

A loud shout and a sudden, furious barking on the other side of her patio wall shattered the evening calm. Kate nearly jumped out of her skin. Wine splashed all over her hand and a good part of her silk blouse.

"Hold still, you blasted mutt."

A series of wild howls accompanied the angry command.

Kate scrambled to her feet, toppling the chair behind her. She backed toward the French doors, trying desperately to recall if there was a poker beside the fireplace to use as a weapon. Before she could pull the doors closed, a hard pounding sounded on the wooden gate.

"Ms. O'Sullivan! Open up."

Kate stared at the gate.

"It's me. Dan Kingman. Open up, would you? Dammit, stop!"

Kate assumed the last command was directed toward the fierce growling, snapping sound coming from over the high wall.

"Look, I can see your lights. I know you're there. Open the gate before this animal has me for dinner."

Reluctantly, Kate headed back out on the now-dark patio and approached the gate. She recognized the captain's deep voice, but wasn't anxious to let in whatever it was he had with him. Pulling the bolt back, she opened the gate a crack, just enough to peer out at the dim figure bent almost double. He was holding a bucking, twisting, growling black shadow.

Kingman pushed the gate open with one hip and backed into the patio area, hauling his captive with him by the scruff of its neck. Kate's jaw sagged as she took in his uniform, or lack thereof. He wore another T-shirt, but this time it was tucked into the shortest, raggedest pair of cutoffs Kate had ever seen.

"Shut it, quick," he tossed at her over his shoulder.

Closing her mouth with a click, Kate shook her head. "No way! That thing sounds vicious. I don't want to pen it in with us."

"Shut the gate," Kingman snapped. "I can't hold him much longer. He's not vicious or he would have bitten me before now. He's just objecting to being held."

Kate blinked at his peremptory tone. Just whose patio was this, anyway? Kingman didn't look like he was about to let the animal go until she complied, however. She slipped around him and his vociferously protesting captive to close the gate.

When the captain released his grip, Kate jumped onto an ottoman while the dog ran around the patio in wild, panting circles. Kingman might not have been bitten, but she wasn't taking any chances.

After several mad circuits, the animal finally planted itself in front of the gate and began to scratch at the wood with one paw, howling all the while.

"For heaven's sake, let it out," Kate shouted.

Kingman moved to stand next to her shaky perch, his eyes never leaving the dog. "No. He'll settle down," he yelled back. "I think he's a stray."

"So why did you haul it in here?"

"What?"

"Why'd you bring him in here?"

Kingman shook his head and pointed to his ear. Exasperated, Kate in turn gestured toward the French doors.

He nodded, then reached up and swept her into his arms. Too astonished to protest, Kate felt his hard muscles bunch under her back and legs as he carried her into the living room. He kicked the door shut with one heel before he let her slide, half-indignant and wholly flustered, from his arms.

"Whew, he sure can sound off." Kingman turned to peer out the door.

Kate croaked out an unintelligible sound, then swallowed and tried again. "Would you mind telling me what you were doing outside my patio? And why did you haul that thing in here?"

Kingman turned, and for the second time in two nights Kate found herself face-to-face with an endless expanse of chest. Tonight it was covered in navy cotton, with APD stitched in gold letters over the pocket. Damp patches plastered the thin fabric to his body. Kate swallowed as her fascinated gaze dropped from his chest, past the cutoffs, and down legs covered with dark hair and corded with muscles. His running shoes looked as if they'd been left out in the rain for several weeks. Across the short distance separating them, she could smell the faint tang of healthy male sweat. She shook her head to dispel her sudden, overwhelming awareness of the man and tried to absorb his words.

"I was running in the open area along the mountains and decided to swing by to check on your patio gate. Just wanted to make sure it was locked." A rueful smile tugged at the thick brush of hair on his lip. "I got a little excited when I saw shadows moving in the scrub outside your patio wall and, uh, attacked. The hound resisted arrest."

Kate stared at him in confusion. "You came by to check my gate?"

"Thieves have been known to hit the same place in quick succession."

"So you came by to check my gate?" Kate repeated foolishly, still confused by his unexpected presence and the continual howls vibrating the glass planes of the French doors. She leaned her shoulders against the wall and struggled for a semblance of poise.

"Yeah, well, with you living alone, I thought it wouldn't hurt."

"Didn't we cover that subject last night?" she began, her eyes narrowing. "No, never mind! Look, Captain Kingman, I appreciate your concern. I really do. But—"

"We're just here to serve, ma'am," he interjected with a gleam in his eyes that disarmed Kate completely. She pushed her shoulders off the wall and edged away from him. Suddenly she felt the need for a little space, and a lot of air.

"There was no need for you to come by. Really, I learned a lesson last night. I'm more cautious now. A locksmith's coming tomorrow to change all the locks. And the security folks are coming out, as well, to show me how to use the alarm system."

"Good." He nodded. He started to say something else, only to be interrupted by a particularly loud, long yowl.

"Good grief," Kate exclaimed. "He sounds like he's auditioning for the Met!" Her lips curved in a reluctant smile as the howl gained in both volume and virtuosity. Her eyes met Kingman's in a moment of shared laughter.

"Why did you bring him in here, anyway? He probably wants to go home. Or meet his girlfriend or something."

"I'm pretty sure he's a stray. I could feel every one of his ribs while we were tussling out there, and his fur's all matted. He doesn't have on a collar, either."

Kate bent beside Kingman to peer through the glass. She could barely make out the deep shadow pacing back and forth by the gate.

"Well, we can't have him howling out there all night. You'll have to take him with you."

"I'm a good three-mile run from my car. I can't tug him that distance, resisting all the way." Kingman gave her a sidelong glance. "I suppose you could call the pound."

"*I* could call the pound? You call them! You captured him."

"Let me check him out again. Maybe I missed his collar under all that fur. Have you got anything to tempt him with?"

With the nasty suspicion that she was going to have a large—not to mention loud—uninvited guest unless she did some fast talking, Kate headed for the kitchen.

"Here, try this," she said, and offered Kingman a piece of meat.

Kingman took the hunk of steak and went back outside. He knelt, hand extended, with Kate peering cautiously over his shoulder. "Here, boy. Come here."

For long moments, the dog ignored them both and continued to pace back and forth by the gate. Finally, Kingman's soothing tones seemed to get his attention. That, or the scent of six-dollar-a-pound filet, Kate thought wryly. The dog stopped and eyed them both uncertainly. Kingman coaxed him with low, soft promises. The dog took one step forward, then another. He hesitated, then reached for the meat.

To Kate's surprise, he didn't snatch it away. Instead, he ate with a strange dignity, bit by bit, from Kingman's fingers.

"Good boy." Kingman stroked the dog's head, then felt his massive neck. "Nope, no collar. And his coat's a mess. Probably hasn't been combed in months. Here, feel him."

"No thanks. I'll take your word for it."

Kingman swiveled on his heels and looked up at her. "Look, why don't you keep him here tonight? He's not vicious, only hungry. See how he's calmed down? Feed him a little more and give him a blanket. I'll come back to get him as soon as I can make arrangements for him."

Kate groaned. She'd seen this coming. "No, I can't. I'm gone all day. I couldn't care for him."

"He's tough, he can take care of himself during the day." Kingman straightened and turned toward her. "Seriously, Ms. O'Sullivan, think about it. He'd be a good watchdog for you until the security system comes on-line. I'd feel better knowing you had protection tonight."

"Some protection," Kate retorted. "A thief would only have to toss a filet or two over the wall to get by him. Really, I can't keep him here."

"If he goes to the pound and isn't claimed in three days, they'll put him to sleep. Come on, lady, you don't want this old boy to be put down, do you?"

Kate bit her lip and glanced from Kingman's hazel eyes to a pair of soulful dark ones. She tried to protest once more, but knew before the words were even out of her mouth, they were only a token protest. She couldn't stand the thought of any animal being put to sleep.

A half hour later, as she wiped soap out of her eyes for the third time, she muttered something decidedly uncomplimentary about a certain police captain. From a mound of bubbles deep in her oval bathtub, a pink tongue darted out to take a swipe at her cheek.

"Ugh! Stop it, you dumb mutt. Just keep still. You're only going to be here a day or two, but at least you'll be clean when you leave. Now stop it!"

Two

Dan Kingman drove through the dark streets, thinking of the woman he'd just left. He chuckled as he remembered his last view of her, standing on the patio with both hands on her hips, enumerating all the reasons she couldn't keep the animal. He'd known she'd cave in, though. He'd seen the laughter in those incredible eyes at the dog's antics and guessed she wouldn't have the heart to toss the stray out on its ear.

His chuckle deepened when he thought of how she would've tossed *him* out if she'd known the real reason he'd decided to take his run in the Heights this evening. Somehow he suspected she wouldn't buy the fact that her sparkling eyes and long legs had interested him as much as whether or not she'd locked the gate. He wasn't quite sure he bought it himself.

Still, if the dog hadn't provided an excuse to barge in on her tonight, Dan knew he would've found some other reason to knock on her gate. He shifted on the worn leather seat, more than a little surprised at his sudden fascination with Kathleen O'Sullivan. At thirty-nine, he'd been around long enough to know first attractions rarely survived the light of morning. He'd also learned the hard way that he and stubbornly independent women didn't mix. His brief marriage had taught him that.

Yet Dan's first impression of Kathleen on the night of the robbery had teased at him throughout the day. Standing in the open door, silhouetted by the hallway lamps, she'd been a sight to spark any man's interest. Those long legs seemed to go on for miles, leading up to generously curving hips and small, high breasts. Her hair was a wild mass of red-brown waves, framing those remarkable violet eyes. So what if her nose was a little short and her chin tended to tilt at a determined angle? When she smiled, the sum of all her parts added up to one damned attractive female. And one very stubborn one, he reminded himself.

He tried without much success to push the image of the delectable Ms. O'Sullivan from his mind as he showered, then drove across town to a buddy's house. He decided that a night of poker and the companionship of his rowdy friends from the department was what he needed to ease the tightening in his lower body every time he remembered the husky timbre of her voice.

"Hiya, Chief. Sorry about the call last night."

Dan shot his assistant a disgusted look and settled into the creaking wooden chair behind his desk. "You sure have rotten timing, Peters. I had to throw in a full house."

The younger man shrugged, a smile on his lips. He knew from experience the captain's bark was worse than his bite . . . most of the time.

Dan waved him to a chair. "Let's go over what we have on last night's homicide. Then I want to review the status on the Sandia Heights break-ins. The mayor is giving me a real ration on that case."

"Just because he and most of his influential backers happen to live up in the Heights, the guy wants the case cracked like yesterday," the younger man commiserated.

"Politics is politics," Dan replied with a shrug.

The new mayor had campaigned on a platform of cleaning up crime and gang activities. So far he'd been less than pleased with the police progress on a number of cases. And very vocal about the Heights robberies.

An hour later, the two investigating officers assigned to the robbery case eased themselves into chairs in front of Dan's desk.

"Okay, troops, let's have it. Where are we on this?"

"We're close, Captain. The car in the chase belongs to a Dr. Henry. He was out of town yesterday and we couldn't get to him until this morning. Seems his son had the vehicle out the night of the break-ins. We brought the kid in for questioning. He's tough, but scared."

"Good. The juvenile division will know how to handle him. Keep on it. Let me know as soon as you find out anything."

Dan swiveled around in his chair when the two men left and stared out the window of his fourth-floor office. The morning sun was still hanging low behind the Bernallilo County Courthouse just across the street, leaving most of City Plaza bathed in rich violet shadows. Dan propped his feet up on the sill, studying the shifting patterns. He decided he was becoming very partial to that particular color, especially when it stared out at him from a pair of wide, sparkling eyes.

Giving in to a sudden impulse, he pulled the notepad out of his pocket and flipped through the crumpled pages until he found the phone number he was looking for. Settling the phone in his lap, he punched in the numbers.

"Phillips Lab, Scientific Computing Department," a crisp, young voice answered on the first ring.

"Ms. O'Sullivan, please. Tell her it's Captain Kingman, Albuquerque Police Department." Dan waited, his eyes on the gray wall opposite him, his mind on the woman he'd last seen trading doubtful glances with a large, scruffy hound.

"When are you coming to get the dog?" Her low, throaty voice interrupted his musing.

"Good morning to you, too, Ms. O'Sullivan."

After a short pause, she recovered. "Good morning, Captain. When do you intend to pick up your adopted son?"

"That's what I'm calling about. We had a little murder here last night. Just your routine domestic squabble and drug-induced shooting. I'm afraid I'll be tied up for a while."

"What! Look, Kingman, you have to do something about this mutt today. His singing is even worse than mine, and twice as loud. I think his vocal cords never passed puberty."

Dan chuckled into the phone.

"It's not funny," Kate protested. She paused; then Dan heard her reluctant laugh come over the line. "Well, at least I didn't think so when the clock radio clicked on at six this morning and your hound did a duet with Willie Nelson.''

Her laugh was like rich, dark chocolate. Dan felt a sudden tightening, low in his stomach. His feet slid to the floor. Hell, he'd thought he was long past the age of getting turned on by the sound of a woman's laugh. He better put some distance between himself and this woman—fast.

''Look, I'll need a few days to find someone to take him. I'll come after him as soon as I can, I promise.''

''Kingman—''

''I've got to go. The coroner's waiting outside. I'll call you.'' Dan hung up on her indignant protests.

He was still up to his ears in the homicides and an unraveling series of related drug cases when one of the young detectives knocked on his door the next afternoon.

''We got 'em, Captain.''

The man's excited voice pierced Dan's preoccupation with the reports spread out before him.

''Got who?''

''The boys who've been knocking off the homes in the Heights.''

''Tell me,'' Dan ordered, hiding his smile as he waved the man into his office. Sergeant Alvarado had just been promoted to detective a month ago. This was his first case with any high-level interest, and his eagerness to wrap it up showed.

''The kid driving the car wouldn't talk at first, but he finally gave us the names of the boys who were with him during their joyride the other night. We went visiting, and hit pay dirt at the second house. The kid wasn't home, but his mother took us out to the garage. Said she'd just found a stereo and video camera hidden under some boxes. She was afraid her son had gotten into trouble."

"So Juvie confronted the kids with the evidence?"

"Yeah, had each one of them in individually. The youngest finally admitted to the break-ins."

"What kind of evidence do you have, other than the one confession and the stereo?" Dan asked quietly. Juvenile cases were tough. If the evidence wasn't airtight, the judge would throw the charges out in a heartbeat. Even when they had the case sewn up, juvenile offenders would get a break more often than not. Though he'd rather see a youngster get community service and a good scare than a record, Dan thought.

"You're not going to believe this, Captain. They actually videotaped their activities. Made a damn docudrama of every heist. We found the tapes with the stolen stereo in the garage. Only saw the first few minutes of one of the tapes, but it's dynamite."

"Cocky little bastards, aren't they?" Dan laughed and stood to shake the man's hand. "Good job, Alvarado. Give me a copy of the written report tomorrow so I can brief the mayor."

Kate flopped into an overstuffed rattan patio chair with a tired groan. Taking an unwilling, loudly protesting animal to the vet for an exam was more work than she'd ever imagined. Throughout the ordeal, the hound had treated her to a series of hurt, reproachful looks. She'd tried to ignore his accusing eyes, telling herself the exam and shots were for his own good. At least now she knew he was healthy.

Kate watched the dog sniffing around the patio as if he hadn't seen it, much less watered it thoroughly, only an hour before. She sighed when he lifted his leg to drench a small piñon tree. He'd already drowned the yucca in the corner. She'd have to get a first-class land-scaper out to redo the patio before she turned the house back to the owners. The dog finished his appointed rounds and wandered over to sit beside her. With a contented snuffle, he plunked his head in her lap and stared up at her.

"Don't give me any of those wide-eyed, innocent looks," Kate muttered.

Of its own accord, her hand reached out to rub the silky black head. She still couldn't believe how soft and fine his fur turned out to be after it had been washed—three times!—and clipped. The vet thought the mutt had some purebred Labrador retriever somewhere in his ancestry to account for his long body and silky ears. Kate shared a moment of unexpected companionship with the big hound before the shrill of the phone made them both jump.

"Ms. O'Sullivan, this is Detective Alvarado with the Albuquerque Police Department," said a voice when she picked up the receiver. "We think we've recovered some of your stolen property. Could you come down-town in the next day or so and identify the items?"

"Sure, Detective," Kate responded. "I took the af-ternoon off to take…uh, my dog to the vet. I can come down now, if it's convenient."

"Great. Please bring any lists of serial numbers or other identifying records you might have."

Kate hung up and strolled into the bedroom to change out of her jeans and T-shirt, the dog padding beside her.

"That was fast work, Enrico," Kate told him as she pulled on white linen slacks and a loose, silky tunic in her favorite shade of hot pink.

The dog grinned at her, his bushy tail thumping on the thick carpet. She fastened a wide leather belt low on her hips and slipped into a pair of matching sandals. Kate wondered briefly if she should take the dog along with her and leave him in a certain captain's office. No, Kingman might not be there, and then she'd have to make another drive home with Rico trying to convince her he was born a lapdog.

Late-afternoon heat shimmered above the pavement when Kate walked up the steps to the modern, adobe high rise that housed both the Bernallilo County Sheriff's Department and the Albuquerque Police Department. Following directions from the officer on duty at the entrance, she made her way to the Burglaries Branch on the fourth floor.

"Excuse me. I'm supposed to meet with Detective Alvarado. My name is Kathleen O'Sullivan."

The young man at the littered reception desk glanced up. His brows furrowed for a moment, then a slow smile spread across his face.

"Yes, ma'am. You're here about the robberies in the Heights, aren't you?"

"Yes, as a matter of fact. How did you know?"

"I, uh, saw the report."

Kate was surprised he would remember her particular case. From the mounds of papers scattered across his desk waiting to be filed, he must process hundreds of reports.

"Detective Alvarado is expecting you. His desk is the last one on the right." The man waved Kate past the counter to a room filled with long rows of modular desk units. His polite smile broadened into something close to a smirk.

Puzzling over his strange behavior, Kate started down the corridor between the desks. The place vibrated with a low, incessant hum. Phones rang, people talked in groups of two or three at various desks and keyboards clattered at a constant rate. It seemed to Kate some of the activity level died down as she moved through the long room. More than one group broke off their conversation and turned to stare at her. For a moment, she wondered if she'd left the back buttons to her tunic undone or something. She shrugged and stopped in front of the last desk.

"Detective Alvarado? I'm Kathleen O'Sullivan."

The young man jumped up and held out his hand. "Thanks for coming down so quickly, Ms. O'Sullivan. Here, have a seat."

He shuffled through a stack of papers on his desk and pulled out a sheet. "This is a list of property you reported stolen. Here's a list, with accompanying pictures, of what we recovered. I need you to scan it and mark any items you think may be yours. Then we'll go down to the evidence storage area and tag them."

Kate took the lists and spread them out to review. "You do good work, Detective. I'm surprised you solved this case so quickly."

"We were lucky. Got some good leads and nailed all three of the teenagers involved. We've recovered almost everything from the ten houses in your neighborhood that they robbed."

"Good heavens. I didn't know there were ten," Kate commented as she continued to scan the lists. She checked off what looked like her TV and VCR, matching the listed serial numbers with those on inventory she'd had the owners of the house fax to her. On the last page of the list, she found her laptop.

"Oh, great! I'm sure this is my computer. I was just about to buy another one. I can't be without one in my line of work."

She frowned and flipped back through several pages. "I don't see anything on the kachina collection."

"They're on a separate list. Since the dolls don't have serial numbers, we did a special report and pictures on them."

Alvarado spread out a colorful array of photos showing the brightly painted dolls in all their feathered glory. "Good thing we got the tape, or we wouldn't have been able to ID them."

"What tape?" Kate asked absently as she reviewed the pictures. She didn't know much about Indian art, but these sure looked like the little wooden statues that had graced the mantel of her rented house.

"The videotape." When Kate gave him a blank look, the man's professional expression slipped slightly. He hesitated before continuing. "The kids made a video of every place they broke into. Exterior and interior. It's made identifying the stolen property a lot easier."

"Did they make one in my house?"

Alvarado's eyes slid away, as if he didn't want to discuss the tapes further. "Well, yes. They did."

Kate felt a tiny niggle of unease begin to curl in her stomach. "They must've been in the house while I was in the hot tub. I thought I heard something when I got out. Surely they didn't—"

"Good afternoon, Ms. O'Sullivan."

Kate jumped at the deep voice just behind her. She turned to see Dan Kingman, fully dressed for a change. Her mind barely registered the fact that he looked as good in black slacks and a lightweight summer sport coat as he had in cutoffs and T-shirts. She rose from her chair with an unsteady jerk.

Kate's nervousness about the tape turned to absolute, gut-wrenching certainty when she saw the amusement glinting in Kingman's eyes. She took a deep breath.

"Detective Alvarado just informed me that the boys who broke into my house that night made a video."

"As a matter of fact, they did."

"I'd like to have it, please."

"Sorry, ma'am, that's evidence. We can't release it until after the hearing."

Kate clenched her hands on her purse. "Is there . . . is there anything on that tape that . . . I mean, I don't like the idea of them taking pictures in my house. Especially since I was right there and didn't know it."

Kingman took her arm in a loose hold. "Why don't you come to my office? I think we need to talk about this."

As Kate traveled the length of the noisy room beside him, she felt herself to be the target of more interested, amused looks. Kingman barely shut the door of his office before she whirled, her words tumbling out.

"Just what's on that tape?"

"Sit down, Ms.—look, do you mind if I call you Kathleen? I think we're past the Ms. O'Sullivan stage."

"Kate," she said impatiently, her mind on the tape.

"What?"

"Call me Kate. Only my mother calls me Kathleen, and then just when she's about to deliver another lecture on the evils of spinsterhood." Kate dropped into a hard wooden chair. "About this tape, Captain . . ."

"Dan."

Kate ground her teeth. "Dan. Tell me about this tape. What's on it?"

"A scan of the house, inside and out, with a running commentary by one of the boys on what they would steal. Evidently the kid thinks he's a budding TV star."

She let out a little breath of relief.

"And a rather artistic series of shots of you in the hot tub."

Kate closed her eyes. She knew it! Those juvenile delinquents were in her house while she was sitting, blissfully ignorant, in the tub. She'd had a horrible premonition about this tape business as soon as Detective Alvarado refused to meet her eyes. Kate cringed inside. No wonder everyone in the room outside had stared when she walked by. Desperately, she tried to remember how much of herself she'd exposed in the tub. The water bubbled almost to her chin. Surely they couldn't have caught more than a few seconds when she climbed out and pulled that skimpy towel around her.

"I want that tape back, Captain." She managed to keep her voice low and steady, despite the embarrassment coursing through her.

Some of the teasing glint faded from Kingman's eyes. "I'm sorry. It's evidence. I can't give it to you."

Kate swallowed. "It's only evidence if I press charges. If I don't, you have no case and don't need evidence."

All traces of amusement left the face opposite her. Kingman leaned forward. "You've already filed a complaint."

"So I'll withdraw it."

"You can't do that, Kate. We have these kids dead-on. If they get away with this little stunt, who knows what they'll get into next."

"They robbed nine other houses. Use that evidence.
You don't need mine." Embarrassment sharpened her
voice to a curt, angry clip.

Kingman sat back and studied her for a long, silent
moment. Kate refused to look away, although she still
writhed inside at the thought of what must be on that
tape. She blinked when he stood abruptly.

"Let's go get some dinner."

"What?"

"You shouldn't make hasty decisions while you're
upset." Kingman held up his hand when she opened her
mouth to protest. "You have every right to be upset.
Your home was invaded, your privacy violated. You've
had a shock and need something to settle your nerves.
How about a margarita and a serving of the best enchiladas in town?"

Kate tilted her head to one side, surprised at his of-
fer. One part of her mind still worried over the tape.
The other part registered a desire to have dinner with
this man—a desire so strong, it amazed her. Kingman's
image had teased at her consciousness the past few days,
from his disreputable mustache to the way his cutoffs
had displayed a body that belonged in improbable TV
ads for tummy flatteners or other exercise equipment.
Before she had time to gather her scattered thoughts,
Kingman reached down and took her arm.

"Come on, we'll sort this all out at the restaurant.
I'm hungry."

A short time later Kate found herself crowded into a
round booth beside the captain. She edged farther over
on the smooth leather seat to give him more room and
reached out a shaky hand for her frosted margarita
glass.

"Are you okay?" His dark brows knit together in a frown.

"Fine." She took a large, salty gulp. "Why shouldn't I be? I mean, in the last few days I've been frightened half out of my mind. I've been robbed. I've been saddled with an animal who thinks he's Caruso reincarnated. And now I find out I'm the subject of an X-rated home video. What could possibly be upsetting me?"

Kate wiped a finger down the stem of her frosted glass and gave Kingman a wry glance. "Sounds like something out of *The Perils of Pauline,* doesn't it?"

He kept his face straight, but Kate could see amusement dancing in his expressive eyes. In fact, crowded so close to him in the little booth, Kate could see a lot more of Captain Dan Kingman than she could handle. She noted how his shoulders strained against the seams of his sport coat, how the strong column of his throat rose above a loosely knotted tie, how his hair held an almost indiscernible sprinkling of silver among its dark strands. She dropped her eyes and took another quick swallow of her drink.

"It's not really X-rated, you know," Kingman said gently. "More like R-plus."

"I take it you've seen it." Resignation threaded Kate's voice.

"I feel it's my duty to review the evidence in certain cases," he replied solemnly.

"Just how many other people have seen it?" she asked, afraid of the answer but needing to know.

"Only a handful—honest. But word of it spread pretty quickly around the department." He hesitated, then sent her a rueful glance. "I'm afraid you've become something of a celebrity."

Kate groaned and covered her face. She tried to resist when he reached out and pulled her hands down, but with little success. She was beginning to realize that resisting Captain Kingman in anything was next to impossible.

"Listen to me, Kate. I promise you, we won't show any part of the video that's offensive or embarrassing to you in court. We don't need to. But we need to use the part on the burglary."

"Why? You've got nine other tapes. Use them."

"I've worked with Judge Chavez for several years now. She's one of the best juvenile judges I've ever seen, but she's a real stickler. If there are any irregularities, any holes in the evidence, she'll throw our whole case out. I don't want to take that chance."

Kate looked up at him. His eyes were steady, with no trace of the teasing glints she'd seen before.

"Okay, okay," she grumbled. "If you *swear* the damn thing is edited."

The waiter's arrival with a tray of steaming plates cut short their conversation. Kate felt a fleeting regret when Dan's warm hands left hers, but it soon vanished in her enjoyment of the delicious, spicy food. The green chili sauce smothering the enchiladas brought tears to her eyes and made her empty the water glass twice, but she finished every bite. She still marveled at how much hotter New Mexican food was than the variety served in L.A.

With an easy deftness, Dan steered the conversation away from the burglary as they worked their way through dinner. Kate relaxed by imperceptible degrees and shared her impressions of Albuquerque. From there, talk turned to the trials and tribulations of living and working in L.A. Over coffee, she found herself giving him a brief description of her fledgling company.

"So you're a chief executive officer," he commented as he sent the hovering waiter off with a hefty tip and a big grin.

"CEO sounds like a more impressive title than it really is, in a small firm. I'm also marketing director, chief software engineer and head of the personnel department."

He slanted her a thoughtful glance as they walked out into the starry night.

"With all those additional responsibilities, do you think you're going to get this supercomputer all put together and spitting out scientific formulas in less than six months?"

"In less than three," she corrected, sliding into the passenger seat of his car. "I'm already halfway through the performance period of the contract."

"Will you make it?"

"Yes." The determined note in her voice gave way to a rueful laugh. "At least, I hope so. Phase Three depends on it."

The dark streets rolled by, bathed in velvety blue New Mexico twilight.

"Okay, I'll bite. What's Phase Three?"

"I made a schedule for myself when I got out of grad school." Holding up one hand, Kate ticked off each item as she recited it. "Phase One—pay back all my educational loans and settle my mother by twenty-five. Phase Two—enough financial independence to start my own company by thirty. Phase Three—a healthy profit by thirty-five. Phase Four, make the Fortune 500 list by forty."

"What about a personal life in this nice, neat little plan you've laid out? When do you phase in such things as marriage and a family?"

The cool note in his voice surprised Kate. She flicked him a quick glance, but couldn't make out his expression in the dim light.

"I've found you can't schedule or plan on such things as marriage," she replied, shrugging.

"No, you can't."

This time there was no mistaking the edge to his tone. She turned sideways to peer at him. Streetlights illuminated his face in intermittent flashes. It was a spare face, all planes and angles, in keeping with his finely honed athlete's body. Suddenly she was intensely curious about this man who rescued stray dogs and checked up on women living by themselves.

"Enough about me," she pronounced. "What about you? How did you get into the law-enforcement business?"

Although he disliked talking about himself, Dan welcomed the change in subject. Kate's blithe dismissal of marriage and a family had flicked a raw spot in him, one he'd thought long since healed. His wife hadn't wanted a family, either, hadn't even bothered to inform him when she terminated the pregnancy that she decided would interfere with her budding career as a dancer. By mutual consent, they'd terminated the marriage soon afterward.

"I did a stint in the marines," he replied a little stiffly, "then used the GI bill to go to law school."

Kate's gurgle of laughter brought his head around.

"I'm trying to picture you without that disreputable mustache."

"Try without any hair at all," he replied dryly, beguiled by her low, throaty laugh. He pushed the dim, distant memories into the past where they belonged and willed himself to relax.

"How did you get from law school to law enforcement?"

"I decided I didn't like the idea of helping bad guys weasel out of their just deserts because of some minor technicality. So I joined the police force."

Dan filled the rest of the short drive with outrageous anecdotes from his rookie days, as much to hear her low, musical laughter as to eat up the miles. Turning into the department's parking lot, he pulled up alongside her car and switched off the ignition. Sudden, blanketing silence wrapped them. Slewing sideways in his seat, Dan met her wide, luminous eyes and knew what would come next.

"Come here, Kate."

Before the words were out of his mouth, Dan knew he'd probably regret them. His every instinct told him he shouldn't take this woman in his arms. She was bright and ambitious and living according to a schedule that didn't appear to allow for the things he hungered for. He had enough complications in his life without a wide-eyed, long-legged redhead adding to them. Yet even as the arguments formed in his mind, he ignored them.

Slowly, deliberately, he slid his palm behind her neck and tugged her toward him. She leaned forward awkwardly, one elbow propped on the console between the bucket seats, her hands splayed against his chest. Her eyes gleamed in the glow of the streetlights before he lowered his head and blocked out the light altogether.

She tasted of salty margarita and something softer, something sweeter. Dan explored her lips with his tongue and, hiding in one corner of her mouth, found a tiny bead of honey from the sopapillas they'd consumed. Groaning, he deepened the kiss. She responded instinctively, leaning into him, opening her mouth under his hungry assault. When he finally raised his head, his breath rasped in his throat.

"I've been wanting to do that since the first moment I saw you." His admission was as reluctant as it was necessary.

"Me, too."

Her husky laugh sent a ripple of pleasure to every one of his extremities. His fingers tightened in her hair. His toes curled in his shoes. And he forced himself not to think about what was happening elsewhere. Leaning his forehead against hers, he drew in a deep breath.

"You taste good," he murmured.

"You, too," she whispered, lifting her face for another kiss.

Dan tangled his fingers in the soft mass of her hair, while his other hand slid slowly down to shape her hip. Her tongue began a sensual dance with his that left him wanting more. Much more. A hungry ache curled low in his belly.

When Dan leaned back, his breathing harsh in the quiet darkness, Kate felt a sense of loss that surprised her. She hadn't reached her advanced age without being in love once or twice, or at least without thinking she was. But she hadn't ever experienced so quickly such desire for anyone—not even her unlamented ex-fiancé.

She was still trying to sort out her confused feelings when Dan opened his door, then came around to hers.

"Come on, Kate. Let's get you home."

With a definite sense of regret, she slid out of his car and headed for her own. She could feel Dan's presence behind her as she fumbled with the keys. When the door opened, she turned back to the man looming behind her.

"Thanks for dinner," she told him softly.

"Thanks for *after* dinner." He smiled down at her.

She could see the stark whiteness of his teeth gleaming under that bushy mustache. Unconsciously, she licked her lips, remembering the way the soft, springy hairs had rubbed against her mouth.

Dan gave a little groan and took her in his arms. There was nothing gentle about his kiss this time. This time it was hard and hot and hungry. His tongue demanded entry, and she gave it willingly. He widened his stance, shifting Kate into the cradle of his thighs. She clung to him, off balance, feeling the hard evidence of his desire.

To her chagrin, it was Dan who lifted his head and drew in a deep, steadying breath.

"Any more of this and we won't make it out of the parking lot." His thumbs brushed her cheeks in tender feather-light strokes. "I'm too darned big to fit comfortably into the back seat of a car. And from what I've seen of that long, luscious body of yours, you wouldn't fit, either. But you better get home, before we put it to the test."

Kate gave a shaky laugh and had turned to slide into her car when his words penetrated her lingering pleasure. Slowly she faced him again.

"What do you mean, from what you've seen? Are you referring to that videotape?" A tiny hurt formed deep in the pit of her stomach. "Is that what this was all about, Dan? This big romantic scene?"

She frowned, the hurt spreading and changing to embarrassment when she thought of how she'd all but melted in his arms. First that damn tape, now her unabashed eagerness for his kisses. Kate refused to articulate, even to herself, what the man must think of her. She got into her car and started to slam the door.

Dan's strong hand held it open. He leaned down, trying to see her face in the dim light, but Kate kept her face turned away. She'd already exposed far too much to this man, literally and figuratively.

"Kate, listen to me. I kissed you because you're a lovely, desirable woman. It doesn't have anything to do with that tape."

"Look, I really don't want to talk about this anymore. I've got to go." She shoved the key in the ignition and gunned the engine. Suddenly she needed to get away from this overwhelming, disturbing man.

"Dammit, you can't think I came on to you because of that tape. Kate, please, we need to talk about this."

"No, we don't. What I need is to put this whole embarrassing episode out of my mind and my life. Let go of the door, Kingman."

Kate breathed a sigh of relief when he stood back and let the door slam shut. She started to drive off, then braked to a quick stop. Pressing the button to open the window, she leaned out to yell back to him.

"And come get your dog!"

Three

"**D**ammit, Kate, don't hang up again. This is official business." Dan held his breath through the long pause that followed.

"I told you the last two times you called I don't want to see you again, Captain. Except when you come to pick up the hound."

Dan gripped the phone, hard. "Look, Kate, I know you're embarrassed about that damn tape, but you have to put it aside. We have a complication on the burglary case. I need to talk to you."

"So talk."

"It's too complex to handle over the phone. Can you come down to the office?"

"No, I'm busy."

Gritting his teeth, Dan swallowed his initial retort. When Ms. O'Sullivan got her Irish up, it stayed up.

"All right," he managed. "I'll come out to the base. What building are you in?"

Kate hung up before he'd even jotted down the building number. Dan restrained his own impulse to slam down the receiver. Detective Alvarado was sitting across the desk from him. He'd already witnessed Dan having to call Kate back after the two times she'd cut him off. No need to let the young sergeant know how much the stubborn woman got to him. Dan's chair groaned in protest as he leaned back to survey the man opposite him.

"Are you absolutely sure none of the other nine victims will take this on?"

Alvarado shook his head. "I've contacted each of them personally, Captain. Some I talked to twice, after I got the word from the juvenile caseworker. Ms. O'Sullivan is our last hope."

Dan shook his head and pulled the folder Alvarado had laid on his desk toward him.

"I would've called her myself," the detective continued, "but I thought you might have more influence with her since you...dealt with her when she was down here last week."

Dan glanced up to meet Alvarado's bland look. He knew darn well what thoughts were churning behind the man's impassive face. There weren't any secrets in the APD. The morning after his dinner with Kate, Dan's assistant had greeted him with a cup of coffee and the previous night's reports. He'd also mentioned that a couple of patrolmen going off-duty had seen a certain officer of the law putting the make on a tall, leggy redhead in the parking lot the evening before. The story was all over the department, his assistant mentioned casually. And the woman had already been ID'ed as the star of the videotape they'd all heard rumors about. Dan suspected the fact that the same woman had just hung up on him would make the rounds of the entire division within hours.

"I'll do my best to convince her. Now get out of here so I can study these profiles."

Dan spread the neat files out in front of him. He picked up the top one and studied the boy it documented. Only fifteen, a good student, son of a prominent University of New Mexico professor, residence in Sandia Heights.

The second suspect was sixteen, from a less privileged family in the valley. No father listed at home, mother worked nights, previous pickups for drug use and petty theft. A known gang member.

The third file was the one that held Dan's attention. Jason Stone, eleven years old, parents dead. An older brother just out of the county detention center for armed robbery, busted parole—present whereabouts unknown. Jason had one previous pickup for running away from his foster home and roaming the streets late at night. The photo attached to the file showed a towheaded kid with wide, scared eyes. Dan folded the file, slipped it into his jacket pocket and headed out of his office.

Driving out to the base, he wondered how he'd break down the barrier Kate had erected between them. He also wondered why it was so darn important to him to do so. He'd thought about her all week, becoming irritated, then frustrated when she wouldn't take his calls. He told himself she was all wrong for him. She was too wrapped up in her job to have time for him, too eager to finish her project and head back to L.A. for anything to come of the sizzling attraction between them.

But his pulse started to speed up as he passed through the sandstone front gate of Kirtland Air Force Base.

"Look at him, Kate. He's just a kid."

"I know, I know! But I just don't want to get involved."

"He's only eleven years old. This is the most serious trouble he's been in. If someone doesn't help him now, he could end up like his older brother, with a record of serious offenses."

"I can't, Dan. I'm embarrassed enough by this whole thing. I couldn't face this kid, knowing he spied on me like that." Kate paced the small office she'd commandeered for privacy.

Dan had to admire the picture she made, despite her agitation. In a calf-length skirt in a swirling pattern of greens and blues and a sapphire-colored shirt of some soft, slinky-looking material, she looked glowing and vibrant. She'd even tamed that mane of hers into a sleek braid that hung down between her shoulder blades.

"I'm sorry, I just can't," she repeated, turning to face him.

Dan studied her worried expression and tried again. "Judge Chavez is committed to this program. She believes that our community is too fragmented, too split into haves and have-nots. That people aren't talking to or getting involved with each other. So she supports this community service program for first offenders in non-violent cases. Instead of the juvenile detention center, the offender is given community service under the supervision of the victim. Assuming the victim agrees, of course."

"I can't say I think much of the program." Kate resumed her pacing. "Whoever came up with this idea must never have been on the receiving end of a crime."

Dan felt a tinge of red creeping up his cheeks but kept silent while Kate continued.

"Besides, I just don't have time. My schedule on this project is too tight. You'll have to find someone else."

"There isn't anyone else. The juvenile caseworker has covered the other two boys, but struck out on this one. Everyone's either too busy or going on extended vacations or caring for an elderly aunt. They don't have time to bother with a homeless kid."

"Oh, no you don't!" Kate faced him, hands on hips. "Don't try to lay a guilt trip on me. I'm the victim in this case, remember?"

Dan gave up. He'd learned in the marines when to fight and when to beat a strategic retreat and regroup his forces. He slipped the file back into his pocket, and leaned one hip against the desk.

"Okay, you can't do it. End of subject. Now let's talk about us."

"I don't want to talk about us. There *is* no us to talk about. I told you that last week."

"Yes, and every time I've tried to call you since."

"Well, stop calling," Kate tossed at him.

Dan eased off the desk and moved to stand beside her. "Are you really so angry with me for one kiss?"

"Three kisses," she muttered, then flushed a dull red.

"Okay, three kisses. I know I don't have the world's greatest technique, but I didn't think I was that bad."

His hangdog expression brought a smile to her lips. "Well, I've had better—but not many," she amended hastily as his brows drew together in a scowl.

"Do you still think I was so turned on by that video that I couldn't wait to jump your bones?" Dan asked, tackling the issue head-on.

Kate bit her lip and sighed. "No, not really. I guess my temper got the best of me and I overreacted. This whole situation has thrown me off balance. I . . . I was too embarrassed to face you again, after that damn tape and the way I responded in the car."

Dan himself had had vivid dreams late at night about the way she'd responded.

"Why don't we get back on an even keel with dinner?" he suggested. "Let me take you out tonight. I'll be on my best behavior, I promise. Any bone jumping will be strictly up to you."

He could see reluctant laughter lighten her eyes.

"Come on, Kate. Even hot-tempered redheads have to eat."

"No, I don't think it's a good idea," she responded after a moment. "I'll only be here a few more months. My schedule's just too tight for any socializing. I don't have time . . . neither one of us has time for any kind of relationship."

Dan studied her determined chin. The contrast between the soft, smooth skin covering it and the firm bone beneath fascinated him.

"Not every relationship has to fit into a schedule, you know. Some just happen to develop, all on their own. Have dinner with me, Kate."

Dan sucked in his breath as she took one corner of her lower lip between even, white teeth, totally unconscious of the provocative innocence of the gesture.

"All right," she finally agreed. The reluctance in her voice made him smile.

"It'll have to be late. Around eight-thirty or nine. I have a city council meeting this evening."

"That's better for me, anyway. I'll be here late, as well." She hesitated, chewing on her lip once more. "Look, why don't you just come up to my place. Neither of us will feel like going out that late. I'll put some lasagna in the oven."

"Deal! See you tonight."

Kate was smiling when she punched in the cipher code and strolled into the lab after escorting Dan out. Seeing him face-to-face had helped eliminate most of the lingering embarrassment from their last encounter.

Trish met her, clipboard in hand and a smug grin on her face. "So that's the mysterious Captain Kingman who's been calling here all week, the one you've been palming off with excuses. Not bad, Kate. Not bad at all. I sure wouldn't have put him off." Trish wriggled her eyebrows in an exaggerated leer.

Kate laughed and led the way back to their worktable. "Captain Kingman can be a bit overpowering at times. But I've decided I can take him in small doses."

"Well, however you take him, take him! He looks like a keeper."

"I wouldn't know a keeper if I saw one, Trish," Kate told her, only half joking. "The men in my life have been noticeably short-term."

Trish nodded sympathetically. The two women had shared a little of their pasts over the months they'd worked together. When Kate first hired her for this project, Trish confided afterward how desperate she'd been for work. Her husband had just left her stranded, with car and house payments to make and three kids in school. In this era of layoffs and defense cutbacks, she'd had a hard time finding immediate employment, even with her computer skills.

Her situation had struck a chord with Kate. Her own father had taken off when she was still a child. Kate and her mother had worked hard all their lives to support themselves. Holding down two jobs throughout college and then putting everything she had into her career, Kate hadn't had much time for dating. The few men she'd gone out with hadn't appreciated taking a back seat to her determined career goals, and they soon drifted away. The one man she thought she loved had betrayed her, much as Trish's husband had.

She'd met Charles at a conference on advanced concepts in software development. He worked for a rival Silicon Valley firm, although at a lower management level than Kate. At first he was attracted by her dedication to the business. Then he professed to be captivated by her spirit and warmth. Surprised that such a charming man was so interested in her, Kate soon tumbled into love and a full-blown affair. When Charles gave her a small diamond ring, Kate's mother was as ecstatic as the bride-to-be herself.

It was one of the shortest engagements on record, lasting less than a week. Her mother hadn't even finished calling all her friends with the happy news that her only daughter was *finally* engaged, when Kate discovered her fiancé had somehow neglected to mention the fact he already had a wife. Oh, his wife didn't understand him, of course. She had no appreciation of the stress of this cutthroat business, not like Kate did. Charles swore he'd planned all along to get a divorce. Too hurt and angry to listen to his pathetic pleas, Kate had given him back the ring and refused to see him again. She could laugh about it now, but it had hurt then. Not as much as she'd thought it would, but enough to make her even more determined to carve an independent life for herself. She threw herself totally into her career, then into her fledgling business.

Pushing the unpleasant memories away, Kate leaned over the table next to Trish. Long, computer-generated runs felt smooth and slick under her fingers.

"What have we got here?"

"The first test patterns." Trish traced the wavering patterns with a green felt tip pen. "Unit One is running the test perfectly."

"Great!" Kate exclaimed, her excitement building as she examined the new estimates to completion. "We should have the first unit finished tomorrow."

"Tonight, if we keep at it. Both engineers working the programming are willing to stay all night, if necessary. My mother's got my kids, so I can stay as long as you need me."

Kate nibbled on the tip of her pen. Her first impulse was to call Dan and cancel their impromptu date. Getting this first unit on-line was a critical deliverable in her contract with the air force. If this went well, she'd get the first big installment of her fee. It was all she needed to pay off her small business loan. Future payments of her fee would be pure profit, after operating expenses. And she was ahead of schedule to completion. Tantalizing visions of the future danced in her mind.

"Do you want me to tell the guys to stay, Kate?"

She blinked and focused on Trish, waiting patiently beside her at the worktable. The delicious visions faded.

"No. Tell them to knock off early. We're in good shape and there's no need for us to kill ourselves. I'd rather have everyone fresh and rested tomorrow so we do this first unit right."

As she drove home later through the summer evening, Kate refused to admit, even to herself, how much a reluctance to cancel her date with Dan played in her decision to send the team home. It was true she'd get a better product from a rested staff. In her heart, though, she knew that wasn't the real reason. A shiver of anticipation raised the fine hairs on her arms as she thought of spending the evening with the complex, fascinating man that was Dan.

For some reason, she couldn't sort out her confused feelings about him. A part of her still cringed whenever she thought of the uninhibited way she'd responded to his kisses, like some teenager with hyperactive hormones. At the same time, she had to admit he intrigued her. And attracted her. And *dis*tracted her when she should have been concentrating on work. Even Charles hadn't generated such a welter of conflicting emotions.

That last thought surprised her. After she'd given Charles back his ring, she'd vowed not to get involved with another man until she had achieved her self-imposed goals. Kate frowned, wondering once again just why she'd agreed to dinner. Every instinct told her this man could complicate her life. He was too smooth, too forceful, too damn attractive. She shouldn't have agreed to see him again, she thought. Well, at least she could send the dog home with him tonight. Kate's frown deepened when she realized the idea didn't please as much as it should have.

"Mmm, something smells good." Dan sniffed the air when Kate opened the door.

"My mother's own recipe. She makes pretty good lasagna for second-generation Irish." Kate smiled as she stood aside to let him in.

"No, that's not what I smell."

Dan stepped inside and tugged her into his arms. He bent down to nuzzle his face in her hair. "Just what I thought—gardenias." He leaned back with a smug expression.

Kate laughed. "Some investigator you make, Captain Kingman. It's plain old shampoo and a spritz of Chanel No. 5." She pushed out of his arms and closed the door.

Dan grinned and followed her into the kitchen. "Did you have trouble getting away?"

"Actually, I took off an hour early and treated myself to a good soak in the hot tub."

"I may have to revise my opinion of those contraptions if they give you such a healthy glow. You look— Watch it, mutt!"

Dan nearly tripped over a black, squirming body that wrapped itself around his knees. "Good Lord, is this the same hound I left with you?"

"One and the same."

Kate paused at the built-in bar to watch while Dan fondled the dog's eager head. Even in the subdued living room lighting, she could see traces of fatigue fanning out from his eyes. He wore a dark summer suit, the well-cut lines adding a touch of sophistication to his tall frame. For the first time, Kate could envision him as an attorney. But the shaggy mustache and loosened tie made him all-too-human—and attractive—in Kate's eyes.

"Rough meeting?" she asked.

He nodded absently, absorbed in tugging the dog's silky ears. "The city council is up in arms about the increase in gang-related drug cases. Statistically, we're below average for a city our size, but the trend isn't good."

Dan sat back on the couch, eased his long legs out in front of him and lifted one hand to rub the back of his neck.

"How about a drink?" Kate asked to cover the unexpected pang of concern that shot through her. She was surprised at how much it bothered her that Dan had a tough job, one that put dark shadows under his eyes. She mixed the drink he requested and poured herself a glass of wine.

She watched him unobtrusively throughout their meal of crisp, green salad and savory lasagna. He'd removed his coat and tie and the small revolver he wore at his waist. He looked more relaxed as he kept up his end of their light conversation, which ranged from music to books to leisure activities. His tastes in literature were much more eclectic than hers, but they shared a common passion for suspense. Dan made her laugh with his highly embellished, totally improbable plot for the mystery novel he was going to write someday.

They lingered at the table, empty plates pushed aside. As she sipped her coffee, Kate found herself growing more and more aware of the man opposite her. He made the airy, high-ceilinged dining room shrink until she could see only him. Her eyes dropped to his hand, resting casually on the table. He had strong, blunt fingers. Heat crept across Kate's cheeks as she remembered how incredibly erotic those fingers felt against her cheek and hip on that to-be-forgotten night. Hastily she lifted her gaze to his face.

The lines of fatigue around his hazel eyes brought a new wave of concern. When he rubbed his neck once more, she rose abruptly.

"Come with me."

"What?"

"Come on. I've got the cure for what ails you."

Dan got to his feet slowly, a wicked grin lifting one corner of his mustache.

"Not that," Kate told him, laughing. "There, on the deck. A good soak will relax those muscles."

"No, thanks. I'm not into the Southern California hot-tub scene."

Kate grinned at the unconscious sneer in his voice. "Talk about reverse snobbery! The tub has a very therapeutic value, you know."

"I can think of a lot better ways to relax," Dan told her, reaching out to pull her against his chest.

A spark of heat flared in Kate's stomach at the feel of his hard flesh under her fingertips. He was so solid, so warm and welcoming. She resisted the impulse to lay her head on his chest and looked up instead, a question in her eyes.

"I know, Kate, I know. I'm not sure about this, either. But if I don't kiss you again soon, I'm going to regret it."

"Dan, about that night, in your car . . . the tape . . ."

"If you even think about, let alone mention that damn tape again, I swear I'll run you in." He bent down to nuzzle his face in her hair once more. "Ah, I love this mop of yours."

Kate felt something inside of her give a little lurch. Her limited experience with Charles hadn't prepared her for the way her breath caught in her throat when Dan held her. Or for the way her heart seemed to beat double time when she touched him. A tiny voice far back in her mind warned her that she was about to take a dangerous step, that giving in to these swamping sensations would create complications in her life she wasn't prepared for. She lifted her head to stare at him, her lower lip caught between her teeth.

Dan smiled down at her. "Don't worry about it so much, sweetheart."

Kate could see the amusement and some strange, indefinable emotion in his eyes.

"We'll just take it as it comes," he growled softly.

When he lowered his head and covered her mouth with his, Kate stopped worrying. She also stopped breathing. His tongue began to run over her lips, first the upper and then the lower, in soft, sensuous strokes. Kate stood it as long as she could, then opened her mouth to taste him fully. The bristles on his chin rasped against her, sending an erotic, tactile message of raw maleness. This was crazy, she thought, while she could still think at all. Just the feel of Dan's whiskers shouldn't make her stomach clench in hot desire. But it did, and then some!

She barely noticed when he shifted his stance. His hands no longer supported her. They roamed at will up and down her rib cage, then caught the silk of her blouse, half lifting it and baring her skin to the cooled air. When one hand moved around to cover her breast, she started.

"Don't you want me to do this?" Dan breathed into her ear as his palm rested, hot and heavy, on the thin lace of her bra. Kate felt her nipples hardening.

"Hmm, I guess you do," he teased, his breath moist in her ear. His hand resumed its stroking and kneading. She felt his thumb circle the hard tip, tease it, rub it. When he bent his head suddenly and covered the aching nipple with his mouth, Kate gasped. A sweet, burning sensation radiated from her breast. Her stomach clenched as the fire turned to hot, molten lava.

"Wait...Dan, wait," she whispered to the dark head bent over her. He straightened, looking down with a quiet question in his eyes.

"I ... you ... this is too fast! I'm confused. I can't think when you do that."

"That's the whole idea." He grinned, running the backs of two fingers down her cheek. "I want you confused. I want you as hungry as I am. Hell, woman, I just want you. But we'll slow it down until you make up your mind."

With a quick stoop, he lifted her in his arms and carried her back into the living room. He settled them both in a corner of the couch, holding her across his lap with one arm while he pushed the dog off the couch with the other.

"Go find your own female," he told the grinning mutt. "This one's taken."

"He thinks you want to play," Kate told him, nestling deeper in his arms.

"I do. But not with him. Outta here, mutt."

"Go away, Rico," Kate instructed.

Dan paused with his lips only inches from hers. "Rico?"

"After Enrico Caruso," Kate breathed, distracted by the face hovering above her. She could hardly remember her own name, let alone the dog's.

"He loves opera," she gasped, around the tiny, stinging nips Dan was giving her lower lip.

"And country and western."

Dan turned his attention to her upper lip.

"And anything else that happens to be on the radio."

Kate thought she heard a low chuckle before he filled her mouth with a deep, hungry kiss. When she surfaced for air long minutes—or maybe hours—later, she leaned back in his arms. Dan slowly lowered her onto the smooth, cool fabric of the couch, then leaned over her.

"Still confused, Kate?"

Kate looked up at the dark head above hers. "Yes," she whispered. "More than ever. But it's the most wonderful confusion I've ever felt." She wrapped both arms around his neck and drew him down.

He didn't hesitate to take her up on her invitation. One of his hard thighs wedged between hers, rubbing against her center, sending shafts of pure pleasure rippling through her whole body. She took a couple of quick breaths, then turned her hungry mouth back to his.

Her doubts melted under the onslaught of his mouth and hands. She'd never experienced the desire this man was rousing in her with his touch, with his dark, delicious taste. This time it was Dan who pulled back, gulping.

"Much more of this and it'll be very painful to stop."

Kate looked up at the harsh face just inches above her own. Her lids felt heavy with desire. She took a corner of her lip between her teeth, then felt an overpowering urge to bite his. "So don't stop," she whispered.

"Are you sure?"

"Yes."

"No worries about the tape, no angry recriminations?"

"No."

"No feelings of being taken advantage of, no—"

"Look, do you want to do this or don't you?" Kate asked, exasperated. She would have struggled up if the man wasn't sprawled on top of her, weighing her down.

"Yes, ma'am, I surely do." Dan laughed at her indignant face, then covered her mouth again. His sure fingers removed her clothes and his own shirt before he had to get up and haul the pesky, inquisitive dog into the bedroom. Kate lay still, watching him through half-closed eyes. He looked like an ad for a runner's magazine. Sleek muscles roped his arms and shoulders, and his broad back tapered down to a narrow waist. He moved with a lithe, casual grace that belied his height.

Returning, he stretched out beside her and curled her into his arms. One hand held her cradled, the other pushed down the lacy fabric of her bra and stroked her nipple with a teasing touch. He played with her breasts, testing their shape, tantalizing their sensitive peaks.

Kate felt the feather-light touch in parts of her body she never realized were connected to her breast before. And when he bent to take one taut bud in his mouth, she gasped, arching under him.

A red tinge crept up his cheeks and his breathing quickened. Shifting her on the narrow couch, Dan pulled her body beneath his. He nudged her legs apart with one knee. His hand slid between her legs, cupping her mound, then stroking the tight, hot bud it protected. Kate bit down on her lower lip, hard, as moistness gathered at her core.

"Are you protected?"

His low, rasped question barely penetrated Kate's utter absorption in the sensations his hand was producing. She looked up at him blankly for a moment, then shook her head.

He swore, low and succinctly and crushed her against his chest. "Me, neither."

Hot, searing disappointment flooded Kate's veins, warring with a perverse pleasure that he didn't carry an emergency supply of condoms. Somehow the thought that he hadn't planned to go this far helped her bring her whirling senses under control.

"You're mashing me to a pulp," she murmured against his chest when he seemed disinclined to move. His arms loosened, and she sucked in a quick breath. "And you've probably given that dog a complex. He's not used to being shut up. If there are any wet spots on the rug, you've got clean-up duty."

Dan shifted and rolled to a sitting position. Taking her hand, he pulled her up beside him. One hand brushed the tangled hair back from her face.

"I'm sorry about this, Kate. I won't be so unprepared next time."

Embarrassed, Kate could only shake her head.

"Oh, yes, there'll be a next time."

His low promise sent shivers down her spine. A loud, ear-shattering howl prevented her from having to respond, which was fortunate because she didn't know quite what to say to the utter certainty in his eyes. Dan shook his head and went to release the indignant prisoner.

Kate used the few moments respite to pull on her blouse. She'd just slipped the last button into its loop when an ecstatic Rico came bounding out of the bedroom. Knowing it was useless, she didn't try to hold him off. Instead, she wrapped her arms around his thick neck and absorbed the force of his greeting against her body.

"Are you sure you want me to take him away?"

Kate held the wiggling dog in a firm grip as she looked up to find Dan watching them both. Her breath caught at the sight of him. He leaned casually against one wall, arms crossed over his chest, pants slung low on his hips. His hair was rumpled and standing up in spikes. She felt a deep, primal urge to go to him and smooth it down.

The intensity of the feeling startled her. To cover her confusion, she buried her face in Rico's silky fur. The dog's squirming reminded her she had yet to answer his question.

"Where would you take him?"

"Well, I could keep him at my place until I find someone to give him a home. But I have a second-floor apartment, with only a small balcony. No place for him to go during the day."

Kate buried her face in the soft, silky fur. "I guess you better leave him here until you find someone. Just make sure you do though," she warned.

Dan grinned and came back into the living room to finish dressing. "Yes, ma'am. I'll give it my top priority."

"Sure you will. After your murders and drug heists and bank robberies. I have a feeling he's going to be with me for the duration." Kate propped her chin on Rico's convenient head and watched Dan pull on his shirt. She felt a definite sense of regret when the now wrinkled cotton covered his torso.

"Speaking of robberies," Dan said as he buckled his belt, "the hearing on your case is next week."

"So?"

"So you'll have to be there."

"Me? Why? I gave you my statement. You've got the evidence—which *you promised* to edit."

He held up his hands, palms out. "It's done, it's done."

He came and sat beside her on the couch. Kate and Rico found themselves scooted aside to make room for him. Both of them arched under his hand to be stroked, first her neck, then the dog's ears.

"The judge wants the victims there. Detective Alvarado will call you with the time."

Kate swiveled out from under his hand. "I still don't understand why I have to be there. I didn't see anything. It's not like I can identify the kids. I can't add anything that's not already in the sworn statement."

"So tell it to the judge," Dan mocked her gently. Before she could protest further, he slid his hand around her neck and pulled her to him. He rested his forehead against hers and rubbed noses.

"Thanks for dinner, Kate," he whispered.

"Thanks for *after* dinner," she whispered back, laughing.

Four

Kate shifted uncomfortably on the hard wooden bench. She tried not to stare at the three boys with their respective parents scattered along the long hallway outside the hearing room, but her gaze returned to them time and again. The youngest in particular drew her attention. He sat on a bench down the hall, sandy-haired, with a half frightened, half defiant expression that hadn't changed in the hour they'd been waiting. Sitting next to him was a small, dark-haired woman—his foster mother according to Detective Alvarado. An irritated frown marred her face, as if the whole proceeding constituted a personal annoyance.

Just looking at the youngsters made Kate nervous. The thought of them spying on her still raised goose bumps. She avoided the first boy's eyes when he was called into the hearing room, but couldn't help noticing his chastened, apologetic air. His father and the lawyer who entered the room with him must have told him to show the proper remorse, Kate decided.

Evidently the judge didn't buy his act. The boy looked shaken when he and his escorts came out of the hearing room some time later. Detective Alvarado was right behind them, taking advantage of the break in the proceedings to slip outside for a stretch. Recognizing Kate, he strolled over to stand beside her.

"Well, that's one kid who won't have much time to get into trouble for the next six months." He nodded to the group leaving the juvenile courthouse. "The judge gave him a blistering lecture and a hundred hours of community service."

"What kind of service?" Kate asked.

"One of the victims is a doctor who volunteers Saturday mornings at a free clinic. The kid will perform janitorial duty at the clinic under the doc's supervision."

Alvarado broke off as the bailiff called the next boy and his sponsor, a tough-looking air force colonel with a rack of ribbons on his chest.

"If the colonel can't straighten that kid up, no one can." Alvarado chuckled as he got to his feet and headed back into the courtroom.

Kate shifted again and crossed her legs, trying to find a comfortable position on the hard seat. A sharp movement down the hall caught her attention.

The dark-haired woman had the young boy's arm in a tight grip and was shaking him. Defiance edged out the fright that had darkened his eyes. From the whiteness of the woman's knuckles, Kate knew the hold must hurt, yet the boy refused to either answer her angry whisper or look at her.

"Hello, Red."

Startled, Kate glanced up to find Dan beside her. She'd been so absorbed in the small drama, she hadn't even heard his approach. A welcoming smile spread across her face. They hadn't seen much of each other in the past few days—just shared one hurried dinner, followed by a distinctly unhurried kiss before Dan was called away. Kate felt her heart speed up just looking at him.

Dan slouched down on the bench next to her, tiredness written in the deep lines fanning from his eyes.

"How's it going?" he asked.

"Okay, I guess. Detective Alvarado told me the first boy got a tongue-lashing and one hundred hours of community service. The second boy's in there now."

Dan whistled softly. "That'll keep him on the straight and narrow for some time to come. Did Alvarado mention that the oldest boy confessed that he was the one who took the videotapes?"

Kate shook her head.

"It came out in the formal statements. I thought you might want to know only one of them stayed in your house to tape you. The other two got scared when they saw you in the tub and ran out. The oldest boy hid behind the bedroom door and used a zoom lens."

Even as the familiar wash of embarrassment swept over her, Kate felt some of her tension ease. Somehow, she was relieved to know only one of them had seen her. Involuntarily, her eyes flickered back to the youngest, sandy-haired boy. She started to comment to Dan about the interplay she'd seen earlier between the boy and his foster mother, when the hearing room doors opened once more.

She stood while the small party exited, then waited with Dan until the young boy and his foster mother entered. Kate followed in their wake and settled herself on a wooden chair in the paneled hearing room. Other than the dozen or so witness chairs, the room held only a small table where the boy, his mother and the public defender sat, a worktable for the clerk and court stenographer, and a wide, polished oak desk for the judge. Behind the desk sat a neat, petite woman in a dark business suit. A marble nameplate on the desk identified her as Judge Julia Chavez.

To Kate's surprise, only one other person entered when Dan and she did. Frowning, she turned to Dan.

"Where are the others?" she whispered. "The other victims?"

Dan gave her a puzzled glance, but had no chance to reply.

The bailiff called the hearing into session in a singsong, ritualistic cadence and the proceedings began. Detective Alvarado and the other officers gave their statements; then the public defender assigned to the case pleaded the boy's side. There was no denying the evidence, of course, especially with the tapes, so the main argument for leniency was the boy's age and previous clean record.

Judge Chavez tried to encourage Jason to speak for himself, but the boy gave only clipped, curt responses. No matter how she phrased the question, his only answer to why he joined the older boys in their lawlessness was a shrug and an "I dunno." The one time she elicited a real response was when she asked if he stole for drug money. The boy's blue eyes flashed and he looked straight at her.

"I don't do drugs."

"Then why were you stealing, Jason?" the judge asked once more.

The boy hunched his shoulder and looked down at the floor. Judge Chavez threw a questioning look at the dark-haired woman beside him.

"He just did it for the thrill. He's always bored and giving me a hard time at home."

"Aren't there any school or sport activities you're interested in?" the judge asked, trying to reach the towheaded boy. When he just shrugged, she frowned and looked to the foster mother again.

"I got two other foster kids, plus my own," she responded with a touch of belligerence. "I don't have time to keep them all occupied every minute of the day."

Judge Chavez sat back in her chair and studied the boy for a long moment. She pushed a pair of glasses up higher on her nose to peer through a sheaf of papers. With another frown she turned to the juvenile officer.

"I don't see anyone named to act as this boy's sponsor for community service."

"No, ma'am," the young woman responded. "We weren't able to identify anyone."

"Did you tell them the alternative is the Juvenile Detention Center?"

Kate's stomach clenched at the stark fear that settled on the boy's face for a brief instant.

"Yes, ma'am."

"Are any of the other victims present?"

"Yes, ma'am. Two."

Kate started to simmer. Where the heck were all the others? Feeling as if she'd been trapped into this hearing, she forced herself to concentrate on the ongoing exchange.

The judge suspended the actual proceedings to delve into the issue of sponsorship. The other victim, an executive with a defense-related electronics firm, was questioned first. Judge Chavez's frown grew, and the boy's defiant look hardened, as the man pleaded an imminent overseas trip as an excuse.

"Ms. O'Sullivan?"

Kate held up her hand to indicate her presence.

"I see you're self-employed. Is the nature of your business such that you could find time to participate in this program?"

"No, Judge. I own a small consulting firm that specializes in the integration of computer systems. My hours are long and fluctuate from day to day according to the demands of the job." Kate's eyes flickered to the boy once more.

"I'm willing to work with you on the number of hours and days for Jason, given his age."

Kate swallowed, starting to feel guilty at her own excuses. She tried to remind herself that she was the victim, but somehow that assurance didn't help when she glanced over at the boy again. "I'll only be here a few more months. I'm on a short-term contract at Kirtland Air Force Base."

"No reason why you can't learn more about our city in those few months as you work with this child. Tell me what kind of outside interests you have."

"None, really. My life revolves around work."

"Thanks a lot," Dan murmured sotto voce.

"Are you interested in sports? Running, by any chance?"

"No, ma'am. I consider any form of strenuous exercise a pointless waste of good calories."

The judge smiled. "The reason that I ask is that our annual Duke City Marathon is coming up in September. My husband's chairing the volunteer-coordinating committee. Just last night he was complaining about the thousands of tasks that have to be done. We can use your help, and Jason's.''

Kate opened her mouth to protest, then clamped it shut when she saw a desperate hope flare in the boy's eyes.

"Yes, ma'am," she murmured, accepting defeat with what grace she could muster.

"Good." The judge nodded briskly. Her dark eyes slid to Dan. "I saw you talking to Captain Kingman earlier. Are you two acquainted?''

Surprised, Kate nodded. "Yes, we are."

"Great." The other woman beamed. "Since you're a visitor to town and may not know the ropes, get Captain Kingman to explain the sponsorship program to you. He can give you some ideas on how to work with Jason. After all, this whole community-service program was his idea in the first place. He built it from scratch."

Kate swiveled in her seat, her eyes narrowing as they leveled a glare at the big man next to her. The suspicion that she'd been set up flared into certainty. She started to tell him just what she thought of such underhanded tricks when the judge reopened the formal hearing. Seething, Kate heard her assign Jason fifty hours of service, then close the proceedings. At her signal, Dan went forward to speak with her. Kate found herself facing Jason and his foster mother across the clerk's small table. The busy man passed her a stack of papers.

"Here's the phone number where you can reach Jason at home to schedule your appointments. A caseworker will contact you in the next few days to discuss procedures and reporting. Wait until you hear from her or him before you schedule your first session with Jason. And here's a pamphlet explaining the program."

Kate barely heard the clerk's voice. Despite her simmering anger at Dan, her eyes kept straying to the thin young boy opposite her. After giving her one quick look, he turned away. When the clerk finished, Kate hesitated, then held out her hand to the boy.

"I guess we're partners now, Jason. At least for the next few months. I'll call you next week."

The boy's mother had to poke him before he responded at all. "Yeah."

Great, Kate thought as she walked down the hall of the juvenile courthouse toward the front doors. Just great! She'd come to Albuquerque determined to concentrate on this contract, collect her fee, then head back to L.A. Now her life was complicated by a mutt who rattled her windowpanes every time she turned on the stereo and a juvenile delinquent whose idea of fun was probably knocking off small convenience stores.

Kate pushed the heavy doors open. A driving summer rain hit her in the face and did nothing to improve her mood.

"Kate, wait a minute."

Head down, hurrying through the rain, she ignored the deep voice.

"Wait up."

She had almost reached the haven of her car when Dan caught her arm. She turned, wet, straggling hair slithering against her cheeks.

"I don't want to talk to you right now, Dan."

"What?"

"You know darn well I don't have time to get involved in this community-service program. Why did you set me up?"

"Hey, hold on. I didn't set you up."

"Oh, no? Then where were the other six or seven victims today?"

"How the hell should I know? This is Alvarado's case. Except for one particular victim, I haven't been taking much of a personal interest in it."

"Hah!" Kate jerked her arm loose.

"This is ridiculous," Dan muttered. "Why are we standing in the pouring rain arguing? Come on back to my office and let me dry you off."

"No, thanks." Kate backed away from him, her feet almost slipping out from under her on the wet sidewalk.

Dan caught her as she teetered. "What's going on here, Kate? Why are you pulling away from me?"

"Look, I'm feeling slightly overwhelmed right now with all the new distractions in my life. I've got to sort things out. Just back off, okay?"

Dan's eyes narrowed. "I'm not sure I like being classified as a 'distraction.'"

"Well, it's the best I can do right now." Kate pushed a heavy mass of wet hair off her forehead. "I've got to get back to work. I'll see you later."

"Yes, ma'am, you will," Dan muttered, his jaw tight.

It was still raining when Kate left work late that night. Her clothes felt clammy against her skin in the evening air, although Trish had done her best to help dry them out. She'd whisked Kate into the ladies' room and stripped her down to her underwear. Draping the skirt over one hand dryer and blouse over another, Trish perched on a sink in between, punching the two dryers alternately until most of the moisture was gone. Still, her linen skirt would never be the same, Kate thought as she smoothed the wrinkled fabric.

She shivered as she drove through the rain and darkness, and reached down to switch off the air conditioner. Opening her window a crack, she breathed in the soft, drizzly night air.

Albuquerque's climate continued to surprise her. The days were hot, with heat waves shimmering off the asphalt in clear, iridescent curtains, but it was usually a dry, bearable heat. Not like the suffocating, smog-laden air of L.A. The nights were wonderful, filled with velvety blackness and a breathtaking array of stars so bright and close, Kate was often tempted to reach up and touch them.

Tonight, the rain gave the air a sharp, clean edge. As she rounded a corner and drove up the steep hill leading to her house, the lights of the city filled the rearview mirror. They glittered like yellow diamonds in the rain.

Suddenly, a flashing red light blazed in the mirror, obscuring the city view. Instinctively, Kate glanced down at the speedometer. Oh, no! All she needed to cap off her day was a speeding ticket. Biting back a muttered curse, she drove the last few yards to her house and pulled into the wide driveway. The car drew up behind her, light flashing. Kate fumbled in her purse for her license. She was still rummaging in her leather bag when a sharp rap sounded against her window. She pushed the button to lower the window and saw Dan's dark face above her. Irritated relief filled her.

"That wasn't funny, Kingman. You almost made my heart stop with that red light."

"You were going a good ten miles over the speed limit," he told her mildly, leaning one arm against the roof of the Audi. "You ought to be glad it's me and not the neighborhood patrol."

"So what are you going to do, give me a ticket?"

"Nope, just a warning. And a good talking to. And a kiss, if you've gotten over this morning's spurt of temper."

"And if I haven't?"

"I'll probably kiss you anyway." He straightened, pushing himself away from the car. "Drive on into the garage. I'll follow you."

Kate sighed, watching him head back through the drizzle to his own car. During the long afternoon, she'd worked through her anger over getting involved with man, boy and dog. She was her own woman, after all. If she hadn't wanted to take on the responsibilities of the boy, she should have said so. It wasn't fair to take it out on Dan. Not for the first time, she wondered what it was about this man that aroused such reactions in her. In the brief time she'd known him, she'd run the gamut from irritation to surprise to amusement to blazing passion.

She led the way in through the kitchen, tossed her briefcase on the kitchen counter, and headed for the living room. Flipping on the patio lights, she could see Rico on top of his doghouse, watching the French doors with ears perked and tail wagging furiously.

"Smart dog," she muttered, letting him in. "I pay a hundred dollars for a custom-built house, guaranteed to keep you warm and dry, and you don't even have the sense to get in it, out of the rain."

He pressed a wet, sloppy welcome against her hand, then ran to greet Dan. Hunkering down, the man knuckled the squirming dog's ears. Kate watched, a smile tugging at her lips, as two males dripped all over her mauve carpet. When Dan looked up, flashing her a quick grin over Rico's dark head, she forgot all about the carpet. He looked tired, and wet, and incredibly good to her, puddles and all.

She padded past them both and brought a couple of thick, fluffy towels from the bathroom.

"Here. Dry yourself and your buddy off while I change. Then I'll make some coffee."

Kate quickly shed her wrinkled clothes, then slipped into worn jeans and a loose, butternut-yellow T-shirt. She was back in the kitchen, with its glowing tile counters and oven set in a recessed adobe arch, within minutes. Grinding fresh beans, she arranged a tray with thick ceramic mugs and leftover pound cake while the coffee perked.

Dan settled himself on the living room floor, his back resting against the sturdy couch and the towel beneath him. Rico plopped down companionably beside him, filled with unadulterated pleasure at having his two favorite humans home. Handing Dan a mug, Kate settled into a corner of the couch. He smiled his thanks, took a long swallow, then twisted his face into a disgusted grimace.

"What is this?" he asked, staring down into the mug.

"Decaf. Viennese cinnamon decaf, to be specific."

"Ugh. I thought you were making coffee."

"Don't push your luck, fella. You're lucky you got served anything at all after that little stunt with the flashing light."

"I had to get your attention somehow. You can be one stubborn female at times." Dan set his mug down and angled his shoulders to look up at her. "I didn't set you up this morning, you know."

"Why didn't you tell me this whole community-service program is your baby?" Kate asked, resisting the urge to run her fingers through the thick, black hair so close to her knee.

"Would it have made a difference if I had?"

"Yes. No. Oh, I don't know." She leaned her head against the sofa back.

"I didn't want you to become a sponsor because I helped put the program together. Taking on the responsibility for a child has to be a voluntary act, an act of love."

Kate raised her head, her attention snagged by the flatness in his voice. When he didn't volunteer anything further, she gave a small shrug.

"I couldn't let him go to the detention center. He looked so young and scared, despite his bravado."

"That's why I think there's hope for him. He's still smart enough to be scared."

She eyed him thoughtfully. "You really want this one to make it, don't you? Do you get a commission on every save?"

Dan's mustache lifted in a rueful smile. "In a way. The more of these kids we turn around now, the fewer we'll have stabbing old ladies in the street for drug money a few years from now."

Kate narrowed her eyes, studying his face just below her, intriguing in its sharp planes and shadows. "There's more to it than that, isn't there?" she said quietly. "Why are you so personally involved?"

As if weighing how much of himself he wanted to reveal, Dan spoke slowly, almost hesitantly. "Remember I told you I had a stint in the marines?"

Kate nodded.

"I had a choice—either the marines or jail. Neither alternative was particularly attractive. At seventeen, I had my own gang and was just on the edge of a brilliant street career. Luckily, my first gunnery sergeant took one look and told me he'd either beat or run the cockiness out of me."

Dan smiled to himself, his eyes on Rico's slumbering, snoring body. "I opted for running and ended up representing the marines at the interservice trials for the Olympics. I got beat out by an army grunt, to my platoon's everlasting disgust."

Kate kept still, not wanting to disturb this moment of quiet sharing. Dan lifted his head to look at her.

"The point is, that Gunny cared enough to spend some time with me. He kicked me in the rear, rode me unmercifully and gave me a reason to feel proud of myself. He even got me into a GED program so I could finish high school and college in the marines. I used my GI bill for law school after I got out.

"I could see myself in that kid, Kate. Jason needs someone to help him, just like I did."

Kate shifted uncomfortably. "I never said he didn't. But I'm not sure I'm the right one to help him. I don't know anything about boys, Dan. Or girls, either, for that matter. I'm an only child and stayed at my grandmother's after school while my mother worked to support us both. I've never been to basketball games or...or camp...or cruised the malls. My whole world since puberty has been computers."

Dan laughed and shifted the dog's head off his lap. "Yes, I've been meaning to do something about that." He pushed himself off the floor and turned to grin down at her.

"No, I'm serious. I—"

"Come here, Kate." With one sure tug he had her off the couch and into his arms.

Kate put up her hands, holding herself stiff in his arms. "Dan, listen to me. Maybe we're going too fast. I wasn't kidding this morning when I said I was feeling overwhelmed by all the changes in my life lately."

Dan buried his face in her hair. "I'm feeling a bit overwhelmed, too," he murmured against its thickness. "What do you suggest we do about it?"

"We *should* stop right here and you *should* go home," Kate whispered.

"But?"

"But it's raining, and you feel good. Real good." With a sigh, Kate slid her arms up around his neck. She lifted her mouth for his kiss, then pulled back abruptly. "Are you prepared this time?"

"More than you'll ever know," he murmured, shifting so that his rock-hard member pressed against her stomach. Kate felt a flash of sensation deep in her belly. Her mouth dropped in sheer surprise. She'd never felt anything like the instant heat Dan generated in her.

He took quick advantage of her opened mouth, bending to cover it with his own. His lips were hard and hot and demanding, and the need that had built between them exploded. Kate groaned, wrapping her arms more tightly around his neck and straining against his body. Her breasts flattened against his chest, the nipples stiffening as she rubbed back and forth. Dan's arms tightened, pressing her waist and hips into even more intimate contact.

When she moaned and would have sagged down on the couch, Dan caught her up in his arms.

"Oh, no, Katey mine. No couches or back seats for us. I want you spread out beneath me, with every single inch of that luscious body available."

Dan carried her into the bedroom, whispering dark, hot promises of what he planned to do, inch by inch. By the time he laid her on the thick spread, Kate was in a fever of anticipation. Her blood pounded in her ears, in her heart—in places she'd never even realized had blood vessels. Dan straightened and began to undress. Before he'd kicked off his slacks, Kate had shimmied out of her jeans and had reached for the hem of her T-shirt.

His hands stopped hers. "I'll take it from here, sweetheart."

Dan joined her in the wide bed, keeping most of his weight propped on one arm, a heavy leg thrown across hers. Every nerve in Kate's body screamed at him to hurry, but he took his time. With agonizing slowness, he edged up the hem of her shirt. His fingers brushed the swell of her breasts. Finally, he slipped the shirt over her head. His hand shaped her breast in its lacy cup, kneading it gently.

"Mmm, you're beautiful, Kate."

Kate was well aware that she'd been far more liberally endowed with brains than mammary muscle, but his husky words made her feel feminine and incredibly desirable. She arched and her nipple pushed against his hand, demanding attention. Dan obliged, sliding the bra down so that he could take her in his mouth. His rough tongue sent sharp shivers of fire darting throughout her body. After interminable moments, he shifted his attention to her other breast.

Dan's heavy leg slid between her thighs and pried them apart. Impatiently, Kate tugged his head up and explored his mouth with hers while his hand began a slow, deliberate descent from her aching breasts, down her belly. It closed over her mound, encasing her in hard warmth. With incredible sureness, he stroked her, letting the fabric of her panties add to the friction he generated. One finger slipped past the lace trim to press against her core, then slid inside to test her wetness.

Kate arched as he found her center. His hand began an ancient rhythm, heightening her already spiraling sensations. His tongue picked up the rhythm and thrust into her mouth with hungry strokes. His weight was fully atop her now, pressing her down into the spread, holding her immobile while he readied her flowering body. Kate moaned under his assault and pressed against him, rubbing her breasts back and forth against the wiry hair on his chest. She moved her legs, trying to pull his lower body into hers. He resisted, his hand and his mouth working their fiery magic. When Kate thought she'd scream for wanting him, he finally kneed her legs farther apart and thrust into her welcoming wetness.

Bracing himself on both arms, Dan buried his fists in her hair and slanted his mouth over hers. Kate's last thought, before his hands and his hips and his mouth took her beyond thinking, was that this was better—much better—than hot-tubbing.

Five

Kate awakened the next morning to the shrill ring of the phone. Struggling out from under a mound of covers, she found herself trapped by the deadweight of Dan's leg across her thighs. Adding to that immovable impediment was Rico's heavy black head, grinning at her from the foot of the bed.

"Good grief, dog! When did you decide to join us? Get off the bed. Go on." Kate pushed herself up and reached for the phone. Rico wriggled his body a few more inches up the rumpled covers.

"Get out of the bed!" she ordered in exasperation, then gave a flustered hello into the phone.

A heavy silence was her only answer. Kate frowned and leaned back against the padded headboard. "Hello?"

She was about to hang up when she heard her name.

"Kathleen Brigit O'Sullivan! Just who's in bed with you?"

"Oh, hello, Mother." Hunching one shoulder to cradle the phone, she pushed her tangled hair out of her eyes with one hand and the dog off the bed with the other.

"Never mind the 'Hello, Mother'! Who's there with you?"

Kate hesitated, trying to come up with an answer acceptable to her staunchly old-fashioned, Catholic mother. Fortunately, Rico saved her at the last moment. He gave a loud, enthusiastic woof, then jumped over her restraining hand. Kate prayed her mother didn't hear Dan's startled grunt when the dog landed square on his middle.

"Kate, you don't have that dog in bed with you, do you?" Her mother's shocked voice came crackling over the line.

"Not by choice. Why are you calling so early, Mother?"

Another long silence filled the phone. "It's almost ten. Are you all right, Kate?"

"Yes, yes I am. Honestly."

"You never stay in bed past seven, even on weekends. It's one of your least lovable traits, darling."

"Thanks, Mother. Uh, is there a special reason for this call or is it just a social chat?"

Kate felt the mountain beside her begin to stir and decided she'd better hurry the conversation. She wasn't ready to explain Dan to her inquisitive mother. Especially not with him lying next to her naked. Eyeing the large, hairy leg that pushed its way out from under the covers, she vaguely heard her mother's worried voice.

"Are you sure you're all right? You're not sick, are you?"

"No, really, I'm not. Why?"

"Didn't you hear what I just said. Charles called."

"That's nice," she breathed. Another hairy leg snaked out. Kate clutched frantically at the covers as Dan's big hands began to push them down, away from his face—and her chest. She struggled to keep a firm grip on the sheet. It was a few moments before she realized there was total silence at the other end of the line again.

"Ah, Charles called?" she asked, holding on to the sheet with all her strength.

"Yes, you remember Charles. Your fiancé. The one who left you at the altar."

"Not quite at the altar, Mother. We didn't make it that far before he happened to remember he already had a wife." She tried to lower her voice, but to her dismay Dan's dark head turned on the rumpled pillow. His eyes were wide-awake, his black brows raised in interest.

"Look, this really isn't a good time to chat. The— um, the darn dog's being a pest. Why don't I call you back later this afternoon?"

"No, you can't. I've got bingo this afternoon. I just wanted to tell you that Charles called to ask for your address and phone number. He has business in Albuquerque in the next couple of weeks and said he wanted to call you. Said it was important."

"That's nice," Kate muttered again inanely. She tried to push Dan's dark head from her lap where it had suddenly taken up residence. He rolled his head on her belly to give her a wicked grin.

"Yes, very nice."

"Shh," she hissed, hand over the mouthpiece. "This is my mother."

"But I thought you said it was all over between you." Her mother's voice held confusion and just a hint of exasperation. "That you didn't want to see him again. Ever. I wasn't sure I should give him your number."

"What? Oh, sure." Kate barely got out the words. Her breath was caught in her throat. Dan had pulled the sheet out of her clenched fist and was doing things to the bare skin of her stomach she was sure were illegal. "Look, I'll call you tonight, okay? I, ah, really do have to see to the dog."

"The mutt's fine," Dan murmured against her belly when the receiver clattered down a few moments later. "But I could use some attention."

"Dan!" Kate skittered sideways to the edge of the bed. "It's almost ten. Don't you have some bank robbery or something to go solve?"

She finally got one foot planted on the floor and managed to wriggle out of his arms. He rolled over, taking the covers with him, to stand beside her.

"Nope." He grinned as he slid his palm around her neck. "All's quiet on the Albuquerque front or my beeper would have been pinging like crazy. Besides, I threatened my assistant with demotion to patrolman third-class if he bothered me with anything less than a major disaster last night."

"It's morning, Dan," Kate breathed, trying not to blush at what his hands were doing to her in the bright light of day. "I've got to shower and get to work."

"On Saturday?" His dark, stubbly chin rasped against her cheek.

"Especially on Saturday."

Kate eased out of his arms once more and reached for her crumpled T-shirt lying halfway between the bed and the bathroom. It barely covered her fanny, but she felt much better when she pulled it on. She tried not to stare as Dan reached for his own clothes. Maybe there was something to this exercise business after all, Kate thought. Wide shoulders with muscles that rippled in the morning light caught her fascinated gaze. Lean, white buttocks contrasted sharply with the hair-covered columns of his legs as he turned to step into his shorts.

Visions of how those legs had wrapped around her in the dark floated through her mind. Kate gulped and headed for the shower. Her hands trembled as she adjusted the water from warm to cool.

Resting against the slick tiles, Kate let the water wash over her heated body. Memories of the night filled her consciousness, flashing scenes of incredible tenderness and wild passion behind her closed eyes. She clutched her shampoo bottle in a tight hand and held her face up to the water.

What in the world had she gotten into? She'd only known this big, complex man for a few weeks and already she was beginning to crave both his company and his very skilled lovemaking. She swallowed, feeling a flush heat her body even under the cool spray. Was that all it was, just sex? She smiled to herself. No, there was no way she would label what they had shared as "just" sex. There was nothing "just" about it.

But what was it, then? Kate asked herself again, lathering her hair into a pile of rich bubbles. And where could it—whatever "it" was—go? After all these years of struggling, she was finally her own boss and on her way up. She had her future planned almost to the day for the next few years. Where and how would Dan fit into her scheme? Assuming he wanted to, Kate told herself with a slight shock. Dan hadn't given any indication he was interested in anything more than a physical relationship. Kate's lingering pleasure from the night before began to ebb, and a distinct wariness edged its way into her consciousness.

By the time she'd finished her shower and dressed, unease and doubt had nibbled away the last of her pleasure. She walked into the kitchen to find Dan sitting at the counter, grimacing into his coffee mug.

"I'm going to have to get you some decent coffee. I need something stronger than this stuff to get me going in the mornings."

Kate walked around the counter to pour herself a cup. Cradling it in both hands, she leaned back against the stove and surveyed the man sitting so calmly across from her. "Do you plan to spend many mornings here?"

Dan raised his brows. "As many as I can."

Kate took a quick sip. The hot, rich coffee gave her courage. "We need to talk about that. I told you last night I thought this was all going too fast."

"So you did," Dan agreed, a smile cutting through the dark stubble of his chin and cheeks. "And then the pace picked up even more."

Kate felt heat rising in her face. "Maybe we both let ourselves get a bit carried away."

"Oh, no—*a lot* carried away." Dan levered himself off the stool and crossed the kitchen to stand in front of her. "And it was very nice, too, thank you very much."

He reached out and twisted a strand of wet, red silky hair around his finger. Kate looked up to find a rueful smile lighting his gray eyes.

"Don't look so worried, sweetheart. I'm not planning to move in this weekend. I know I can be a little overpowering at times. I'll give you some space, if that's what you want."

She took her lower lip between her teeth. "Yes. At least, I think that's what I want."

"Fine." Dan turned and headed for the door to the garage. "Call me and let me know when your first appointment is with Jason. I'll go with you." The door closed gently behind him.

Kate's jaw dropped. A shaft of pure feminine pique shot through her. She'd expected an argument. Or at least a token protest, for heaven's sake. After what they'd just shared, she didn't think he would just...just leave! She stood rooted to the spot, staring at the door, until the dog plopped himself down on her foot to get her attention.

Dan drove through the bright, sunny morning, his fists tight on the steering wheel. He wasn't as calm as he'd pretended with Kate. It'd taken all his professional cool to stroll out, leaving her there looking so delectable in her canary-yellow shirt and shiny auburn hair that he wanted to... A wide grin spread across his face as he thought of all the things he wanted to do to Kate. He'd done many of them last night. And early this morning. But a few definitely bore repeating.

He shifted uncomfortably in the car seat as his body hardened. Good grief, he'd thought he'd need a hot shower, a long sleep and a thick steak before he'd be ready for his next meeting with Kate. Yet every one of his instincts was urging him to turn his car around, head back up the hill and lose himself in her soft body again and again.

The thought that maybe Kate was right about needing some time to cool off flashed in his mind. He pulled the thought into his consciousness, turned it around, dissected it.

No, he didn't need to cool down. What he needed was Kate. He felt the certainty growing in him with every turn of the car's wheels. The woman he'd just left aroused and intrigued him. She was a mass of contradictions—warm and loving one minute, stubborn and in a temper the next. He never quite knew what to expect of her, and the uncertainty was slowly driving him crazy.

He squinted into the bright sunlight as he compared Kate to his ex-wife. He knew with instinctive certainty that this long-legged redhead had worked her way deeper into his being in the short time he'd known her than his wife had in the three years they'd been married. He'd had enough liaisons in the years since his divorce to know that what he was feeling for Kate was special, unique, completely outside his previous experience. Something to be explored slowly and savored.

Dan frowned as another frustration overlaid the physical one that was making him so uncomfortable. How long was left on that contract of hers? He tried to remember when Kate said she'd be done and heading back for L.A. A couple of months at most. And he just promised to back off, to give her space. Great tactics, he told himself disgustedly. The marines would never have taken Iwo Jima with him laying out the battle plan. He wheeled the car into his parking space, knowing this was going to be one of the longest periods of his life. He'd promised her that he'd wait for her call, and he would. But he wouldn't like the waiting one bit.

* * *

By noon the following Friday, Dan was close to breaking his promise. Very close. He'd reached for the phone half a dozen times in the past week. Once he'd even punched in Kate's number at work, but hung up before it rang. He cursed himself once again for his tactical blunder in letting her have her space. As stubborn as she was, she might think that just because he'd allowed her a little breathing room she was rid of him completely. Dan scowled at the phone one more time, then tried to focus on the reports spread out in front of him.

He was elbow-deep in files when the phone rang.

"Kingman," he growled into the receiver, his eyes and mind still on the intricate white-collar fraud report in front of him.

"Hello, Dan. It's Kate."

A surging sense of relief spread through him, even as excitement began to tingle in his veins. The woman's voice over the phone was enough to put him in a sweat. Dan shook his head, realizing he had it bad.

"I'm supposed to pick Jason up tomorrow morning at eight. Do you still want to join us?"

"Yes, but I can't make it at eight. Where will you be?"

"We're going down to Dr. Chavez's offices. He's got all the material on the marathon there and says he can use some help."

She gave him the address in a distant tone. Dan jotted it down, frowning at the constraint in her voice. "We were supposed to use this time to cool off, not go into a deep freeze. What's the matter?"

Kate sighed. "I've had a rough few days. We've encountered some problems getting all the units on-line."

Dan could hear the strain in her husky voice. "What kind of problems?"

"I don't know," she told him, half laughing, half rueful. "If I did, I could fix them."

"And here I was hoping you were going to say you had a rotten week because you missed me."

Dan cursed himself for his bluntness when a long silence stretched out over the phone. He was searching for something smooth to say when she finally answered.

"I did, a lot."

"Good. Me, too. *A lot.*"

Kate laughed softly. Regret threaded her voice when she spoke. "I'm sorry, Dan, I really can't talk now. We should've had this last unit up two days ago. We're going to keep at it as late as we can tonight. I've got to get this last one running so we can start the integration programming next week."

"Okay, I won't keep you. See you tomorrow."

Dan hung up and stared at the phone thoughtfully, wondering what this hitch would do to her schedule. He knew how much Kate was counting on finishing this job early. She'd mentioned a bonus, a pretty hefty one as he recalled. Well, there wasn't much he could do to help her with this problem, whatever it was. He knew about as much about computers as Rico did.

Kate hung up the phone and looked at it thoughtfully. She was astounded at how just hearing Dan's voice sent shivers of desire down her neck. All week long he'd intruded into her thoughts: during work, during the night, whenever she took a sip of her special cinnamon coffee.

The time away from him hadn't helped at all. Instead of clarifying her own feelings, she was more confused than ever. Kate knew she wanted him with a carnal passion that amazed her. In all her thirty-one years, she'd never felt such intense physical desire. Just thinking of the way his hands and lips had explored her body was enough to make her blush a bright red. Once Trish even noticed her flush and asked if she was feeling all right. Mumbling some incoherent answer, Kate had buried her face and her decidedly lascivious thoughts in a stack of computer manuals.

Adding to her stress was the fact that they'd fallen behind schedule on the project. It was only by a few days, but enough to jeopardize the bonus for early completion. For some unexplained reason, the seventh and eighth sequential memory units failed to integrate with the first six. Until they had all nine subunits installed and integrated, the supercomputer was just a box of brightly colored parts of no use to anyone.

Kate rubbed her forehead and went over to the small cluster of engineers hunched around a worktable.

"Okay, let's go over the integration programming scheme one more time," she said with determined enthusiasm.

The next morning, Dan arrived at the medical center a little after ten. He could see at a glance that the problems at work had kept Kate up late. Lines of strain bracketed her eyes and faint blue shadows darkened the skin under them. But even tired and grouchy, she looked good enough to eat. She had on a pair of cutoff jeans that hugged her hips and made Dan break out in a light sweat. Over them she wore a bright red Stanford T-shirt. The color looked stunning on her. It brought out the deep mahogany sheen of her hair and creamy whiteness of her skin. Dan stirred uncomfortably and forced himself to concentrate on the interaction between woman and boy.

Neither one looked particularly happy to be there. Maybe it was dealing with Jason that was causing the stress in Kate's features, Dan thought. He stood in the open doorway and watched the two of them for a few moments. Kate was bent over a long table, sorting through stacks of haphazardly piled papers. Jason stood on the opposite side of the table, idly shuffling one hand through the piles of forms. His face had a sullen, closed look.

"Here, Jason, I'll show you. We have to sort the different forms by category—for the full marathon, the half marathon and the five-kilometer fun run. Then, when the applications come in, race officials can send out just the information each runner needs."

"This is stupid." The boy pushed at the papers. A stack teetered precariously, then slid to the floor.

Dan watched Kate bite her lip in an obvious effort to hold back her temper. "Please, Jason, I'm not exactly thrilled to be spending my morning playing file clerk, either. Let's just dig in and get it done." She bent to pick up the papers and saw Dan standing in the doorway.

"Good, another sacrificial victim. Come on in and help us sort through this mess."

Dan smiled as he strolled into the spacious, brightly lit room. "Hello, Jason. I'm Dan Kingman."

The boy eyed Dan's hand for a long minute. With a show of reluctance, he put out his own.

"What's the drill?" Dan asked, eyeing the littered table.

Kate dumped the pile of papers from the floor back onto the table. "The printers just delivered the various forms for this year's race. Dr. Chavez volunteered his committee to help sort through them and put together information packages for each of the various runs.''

''So where's the committee?'' Dan asked, pulling a stack toward him.

''They start getting together regularly in a couple of weeks. Jason and I are the advance guard, so to speak. We're going to put together the prototype packages.'' Kate gave the boy a tentative smile, which he ignored.

Dan watched a flush creep up her cheeks. She and Jason were definitely off to a rocky start.

''What do I do?''

Kate grinned at Dan in relief. ''Why don't you start with the blue stack, the ones for the full marathon? We ought to be able to make a good dent in those.''

She stood, frowning down at the papers in her hand. ''You know, all this could easily be computerized.''

''So put it on a computer,'' Dan told her as he pulled a chair over beside Jason. ''Here, you take this little pile and I'll take the big one.''

The boy gave an involuntary grin when Dan pushed a towering stack toward him and pulled one about three sheets high in front of himself. Kate snorted.

''Great! At that rate we'll be here till midnight.''

''Paperwork was never my strong suit,'' Dan told her, eyes twinkling. ''Come on, kid, get to it. I've got the worst craving for an extralarge pepperoni pizza. Slave driver O'Sullivan here probably won't let either of us out for food until we get through this stuff.''

''What did I tell you?'' Dan asked Jason in a loud whisper two hours later.

Kate looked at the accusing looks on the two male faces opposite her and relented. ''Okay, okay, we'll go eat. Here, pile the stacks neatly in this box. Anyone who gets so much as one sheet out of order will answer to me.''

When the last of the papers were stored away, she picked up a small box she'd set aside. In response to Dan's inquiring glance, she told him she wanted to take some of the forms home.

''I think I can come up with a simple program to enter the race data with an optical scanner. It would make correlating all the related items, like entrance fees, runners' categories and such, so much easier.''

''For someone who professes to hate exercise, you're sure getting into this race business,'' Dan commented.

''I hate inefficiency even more,'' Kate responded as the three of them walked out of the spacious medical complex into an afternoon filled with bright blue skies and shimmering sunshine. The temperature hovered around ninety degrees, but the dry heat felt invigorating after the coolness of the medical center. Brilliant pink oleander bushes bordering the entrance added a bright splash of color to the summer day.

''Albuquerque at its finest,'' Dan commented, holding his face up to the sun. ''Bet you don't have many days like this in L.A.''

Kate arched her stiff neck and leaned back to study the brilliant, cloudless sky with tired eyes. ''No, not many.''

Dan gave her a thoughtful look, then reached over to take the box out of her hand. ''I'll put this in your car, then we'll take mine.''

''What time do you have to be back, Jason?'' he asked when he returned and opened the doors to his nondescript official car to let the trapped, stifling air out.

The boy shrugged.

"I told Mrs. Grant, his foster mother, I'd bring him home after lunch. No specific time," Kate volunteered.

Dan turned to the boy, standing silent beside them. "Do you have anything planned for the afternoon?"

Jason squinted up, his blue eyes doubtful. "No, nothing special," he finally replied.

"Good. Come on, we'll call Mrs. Grant from the car."

Jason hung back, obviously reluctant to enter the police car. Although it was unmarked, the crackling radios and litter of official paraphernalia in the front seat made it undeniably an official vehicle. Dan knew the boy was remembering the last time he'd ridden in a police car, on his way to the detention center.

"You sit in back, Kate," Dan suggested casually. "I need Jason up front so he can order the pizza. Do you know how to work a portable phone, kid?"

"Sure," the boy said.

"Come on then, let's go. A man my size can only go so long without sustenance."

Kate slid into the back seat, sucking in her breath when her thighs encountered the hot leather, while Jason settled in the front. Handing the boy the phone, Dan told him to call his foster mother first for permission.

"Now call Information for the number to the pizzeria on Coors Road."

"Isn't that on the other side of town?" Kate asked.

"Yes, it is. Across the Rio Grande."

"Why in the world would we order from someplace so far away?"

Dan winked at Jason, still holding the phone in his hand. "So they can deliver a couple pizzas to Petroglyph Park. We're going to have a picnic, then go exploring."

Six

They arrived at the small national park nestled in the shadow of five volcanic peaks just minutes before the pizza delivery van drove up. Dan paid for the pizzas, handed one to Jason and a carton of soft drinks to Kate, then led the way to picnic tables set among a stand of Russian olive trees. Settling in the shade of the silver-green, feathery branches, they spent the next half hour enjoying the warm sun, cold drinks and spicy pizza. Few tourists had braved the afternoon heat, leaving the trio wrapped in a quiet world of their own.

The high mesa shimmered in the sunlight, while far to the east, Albuquerque sprawled in a somnolent haze. Dan slouched comfortably on the hard wooden bench. He felt infinitely better—he had a full stomach, and the woman he was coming to think of as his own sat next to him. Moreover, he could see that the lines of strain had faded from around Kate's eyes.

"Thanks, Dan." She smiled at him. "I needed some fresh air and good food." She glanced over at Jason.

"Yeah, thanks," the boy mumbled around a large chunk of crust.

"Finish up, troops," Dan ordered. "We've got this whole park to explore."

Both woman and boy groaned in protest.

"Do we have to?" Kate asked. "It'll take too much energy to climb those rocks in this heat."

"Who wants to look at a bunch of silly rocks?" Jason muttered.

"I do. You do, too—both of you. You just don't realize it yet. Come on, eat up." Dan gave Jason the last slice and carried the trash to a handy container.

He led them, still protesting, to the entrance. The Park Service ranger on duty handed them a brochure, then Dan herded them onto the walking trail. It led up a low hill toward a mound of twisted black rock.

"Here, read it to us, Kate. We don't want to miss any of the details."

Dan smiled to himself when he intercepted the resigned look Kate flashed at Jason, and the boy's answering half smile. Given the right circumstances, they just might find some way to communicate yet.

His silent satisfaction grew as he watched the two of them clamber over the rocks to peer at the prehistoric figures carved on the black surfaces. At one point, Jason scrambled up a steep incline, then reached a hand back down to help Kate up. Together they explored a perpendicular wall with delicate carving traced across its surface. Kate's deep auburn curls brushed Jason's sandy mop as their heads bent over the rock. The boy ran a finger over the surprisingly detailed, flowing lines of a horse. A man figure ran beside the horse, holding its mane.

"This is fascinating," Kate breathed. "Look, Jason, they almost seem to be moving in the sunlight." She read from the brochure. "'This figure is thought to be one of the finest examples of prehistoric Anazasi rock art. Both horse and man are drawn in representational style and capture the essence of movement and grace.'"

Jason responded with a low murmur, although Dan could see his eyes drawn to the graceful figure.

Dan followed behind leisurely as they explored the rest of the small park. Kate exclaimed over abstract bird figures, running horses and masks of exotic gods. According to the brochure Kate read faithfully, there were an estimated fifteen hundred figures carved into the black basalt rock of the volcanic escarpment. Most were relics of the prehistoric Indians who had camped there, but many were left by Spanish invaders centuries later.

The park was almost closing by the time Dan led them out and back to the car. Kate filled the long drive back to the medical center with more tidbits from the brochure.

"I'd never even heard of petroglyphs before," she finally said, lowering the crumpled paper.

"Now you're an expert," Dan teased. "They're scattered all over this part of the country. You need to take the time to explore more while you're here. You and Jason."

"Mmm," Kate murmured, while Jason stared out the window.

When he drove into the medical center parking lot and pulled up beside her car, Dan instructed Jason to wait a moment. He joined Kate outside the car and put a firm hand under her chin to tilt her face to the sunlight.

"Much better."

"Better than what?" Her violet eyes smiled up at him.

"You look much better with a touch of sun on your face and the lines gone from your eyes. Go on home, Kate. Indulge yourself in that hot tub contraption of yours, then get some rest. I'll take Jason home." Dan bent to brush her lips.

When he pulled back, his heart leapt at the sudden frustration that darkened her eyes. At least, he thought it was frustration. That sure as hell was what he was feeling. Maybe this period of "space" was worth it, he thought. If it put that disgruntled, unsatisfied look in her eyes, if it made her realize how right they were together, it certainly was worth it. Dan just hoped he would survive long enough for Kate to recognize what she was feeling. He'd never thought of himself as particularly aggressive sexually, but this self-imposed abstinence was starting to make him think in terms of carrying his woman off, much as the prehistoric men of the rock carvings probably had.

For a moment, he was tempted to follow her home and relieve their shared frustration. Kate's eyes told him she wouldn't object. But he held back, his arms falling lightly from her shoulders. He'd sworn to give her time, and he would. She'd tell him when she was ready. He just hoped she was ready damn soon. This nobility crap was for the birds.

Dan waited until her car pulled out of the parking lot before he rejoined Jason. The boy was quiet as they drove toward the southwestern sector of town, his eyes fixed on the passing view.

"You know, you should give Kate a chance. She's okay, once you get to know her."

Jason turned to look at him. A sneer settled over his face, making it look oddly old and cynical. "Looks like you've gotten to know her pretty well."

"Can it, kid," Dan told him mildly. "All you have to do is meet her halfway. Use this time to get to know new people, enjoy some new experiences. Believe me, there's a lot more to the world than the gang you were running with."

"Yeah, sure." Jason turned back to the window.

Dan didn't push it. He knew from long experience the chances of breaking through to the boy were fifty-fifty at best. They had about as many failures as successes in this sponsorship program. It would be tough to reach the boy with just a few hours a week spent outside his normal environment unless Jason opened up to it. And the boy wasn't sending out any signals that he wanted change just yet. Dan could only hope that Kate found some way to capture his interest in the next couple of months.

The kid was worth saving. Dan had discerned intelligence and an adolescent defiance in his blue eyes that reminded him all too much of himself at that age. Jason was street smart, cocky, yet hungry, all at the same time. If they could just feed that hunger, just spark something that interested him. If anyone could, Kate could, Dan thought. She threw herself heart and soul into a project once committed to it.

Dan grinned as he thought of the plush doghouse sitting in solitary splendor in her once-green patio garden. And the box of papers Kate was taking home so she could computerize the marathon details. And the way she had given herself so passionately to his hungry mouth and seeking hands. No, the woman didn't do anything halfway.

Dan glanced over at the still, silent Jason. If anyone could reach the boy, Dan was convinced Kate could.

"I just can't get through to him, Trish."

Tricia nodded absently, her eyes on Kate's plate. "You've only had a couple sessions with the boy so far. Give it time."

"I don't have much time. Only a few hours each weekend."

"Well, you can't expect miracles in just a few weeks. The kid hasn't had a home or family to care for him in years, from what you've told me. You're going to have to work to win his confidence."

The small blonde broke off to shake her head in unabashed admiration as Kate lifted another heaping forkful. "You know, you're the first woman I've ever seen finish off a half of a Travis special."

Kate grinned as she demolished the last of a heaping mound of enchiladas covered with crisp, golden french fries. This was Kate's first visit to the K&I Diner and her first taste of their house specialty, named after the truck driver who invented it. It wouldn't be the last.

"Most men who come here can't even eat a half order. That's why they have a quarter- and eighth-Travis's on the menu," Trish commented, her envious eyes on Kate's plate.

All around them the small, crowded restaurant hummed with the sound of hungry people and the air was filled with a tangy aroma of crisp french fries and spicy enchilada sauce. Kate and Trish had stood in line for over twenty minutes before they'd secured a table. The diner was as popular with the military and civilian personnel from nearby Kirtland Air Force Base as with the locals.

"You shouldn't have brought me to a truck stop if you didn't want me to eat like a truck driver," Kate grinned. "I would never have believed this unlikely combination could be so delicious. I'll have to bring Dan and Jason back here. They could put away a full order each."

Kate frowned as she wiped up the last bit of sauce with a fork full of now-soggy french fries.

"I don't know what I'm going to do with Jason. We've had two sessions together now and he hasn't spoken more than twenty words to me, at most. The first session wasn't so bad, because Dan was there, but the last time was awful. He was bored and all I did was pick at him. I'm really dreading our session tomorrow."

She looked at Trish hopefully. "Any advice? Your son is just a few years older than Jason."

The blonde shook her head. "No, not really. Eleven is a tough age. Sort of in-between. At that stage they're too old for children's toys and too young to be preoccupied with dating and the opposite sex. I think sports like soccer or baseball and electronic games are about all my son was interested in at that age."

Kate sighed. "Jason's different. He doesn't want to participate in any team activities. I suggested the programs at the Y, but he shot that down the first day."

"Sorry I can't help you, Kate," the younger woman said. "Enough about this kid, though. I want to hear how it's going with the incredible hunk."

Kate smiled at the irrepressible blonde. Trish had prodded her to go after Dan ever since she'd glimpsed him that one time he'd come to the lab.

"Okay, I guess."

"You *guess?* Don't you know?"

Kate looked down at her clean plate. "No, not really." She sighed. "He's trying to give me the room I said I wanted, but the man's about as subtle as a pit bull. He's more than ready to take our . . . relationship further. He's waiting—not very patiently—for me to make up my mind."

"You're nuts," Trish said decisively. "You know you like the guy. Go for it!"

"For what? I'll be leaving in a few months. And the project is starting to heat up. I just can't afford to get too involved, emotionally or timewise."

"Believe me, for someone like Dan, I'd find both the time and the emotion."

Kate laughed and grabbed the check. "You would. Come on, back to work."

Much as she tried to keep her mind on the complicated flow plans before her, Kate found herself thinking more about her conversation with Trish than about mainframes that afternoon. She finally gave up and headed home, hoping a good soaking in the hot tub might help her unwind.

Relaxing in the warm, bubbling water, with Rico stretched out blissfully beside the tub, Kate tried to understand just what it was about Dan that disturbed her so much. During the infrequent times they were together these last weeks, she enjoyed his irreverent company as much as she relished his skilled lovemaking. What there was of it. The man had taken her at her word and didn't push her. He teased her and took her to out-of-the-way restaurants and kissed her until she was breathless with longing, then left her.

Perversely, Kate had come to resent his restraint. She didn't like this confused, unsatisfied, unsettled state, even if it was of her own making. Her irritation rose, and the hot tub failed to work its usual magic on her. Darn the man, anyway.

She dried herself off, pulled on a thigh-length, silky sleep shirt and settled into her wide platform bed. Her frustration only increased as she thought of how big and empty the bed seemed now, and how small and crowded and wonderfully warm it had seemed when Dan had taken up more than his fair share of it.

She snuggled into the covers, recognizing that this uncertain state had gone on long enough. She wanted Dan, pure and simple. Tomorrow night she'd tell him so.

Kate was still restless and edgy when she picked up Jason the following morning. He trudged down the short walk from his foster parent's weather-beaten house. His usual sullen expression made the lines of his young face appear set and hard. Kate sighed, then pinned a welcoming smile on her lips.

"Hi, Jason. All set for our meeting with the race officials?"

"Yeah."

"I've got the model program all ready to demo. It took a few late nights to design, but it's pretty slick, if I do say so myself. I even rented an optical scanner to show how they can enter the data as it's received from the applications, then correlate it to the other files, like expenses and finish times, and such."

"Big deal."

Kate's jaw clenched. She wheeled the car through the light Saturday-morning traffic toward the medical center and tried to remember Dan's conviction that Jason was worth the effort.

"It's designed to run on little notebook computers. We can enter all the advance information as we receive it. Then the other volunteers can take the computers right down to the finish lines on the day of the race to punch in times. They'll get instant feedback in each category and can even print out the certified results for each runner, if they want to."

Despite her work schedule and growing preoccupation with a certain officer of the law, Kate was getting more and more excited about the marathon. Now just a little over a month away, the pace of preparatory activities had gone from hectic to frenetic. With an expected record turnout, this year's race promised to be the biggest and most elaborate in its ten-year history.

"Just think what a madhouse it will be, with five-thousand-plus runners in all different categories crossing the finish in waves." She glanced at Jason to see if he felt any of the infectious excitement.

The boy didn't even bother to reply. He kept his head turned away from Kate to stare out the window. Kate gave up. They finished the short ride in silence.

Kate's program was a hit with the committee of volunteers who'd come together to manage the big event. She set up her laptop computer and ran through several sample entries, to their rave reviews. In addition to a database that pulled together all the race information, a simple graphics program printed out fancy certificates for all participants, as well as thank-you letters to the hundreds of volunteers.

"Are you sure you don't want to move to Albuquerque permanently, Ms. O'Sullivan?" Dr. Chavez beamed at her after the demo. "In just a couple weeks, you've done more for the marathon than I've been able to do all year. The race director will love this program.

I've told him what you were working on and he wants to meet with you himself, at your convenience.''

"Anytime." Kate laughed. "I have to admit, I'm starting to get as excited as the rest of you about this race.''

"Well, we sure appreciate your work. Come into the other office. I'll show you the bookkeeping files used last year so you can adapt them to the computer.''

"Sure." Kate turned to the boy standing to one side. "Jason, why don't you put the folding chairs away and start opening the envelopes with the first applications. We'll test-input a few of them when I get back.''

She spent nearly an hour with Dr. Chavez, trying to sort through last year's finances. The volunteer who'd managed the books was a professional accountant and used a sophisticated program much different from the one she employed in her own small business. By the time she'd run through it and wandered back into the reception area, Kate had a more thorough grounding in the race finances than she'd ever wanted. She stopped abruptly when she saw Jason seated at the long table, punching the keyboard of her laptop with busy fingers.

"What are you doing?''

The boy slipped quickly out of the chair. Kate went over to scan the small screen.

"Oh, no," she groaned. "You've erased the templates. And I was in such a rush I didn't back up the last couple.''

"So?" The boy's low, defiant ton´ almost shredded Kate's volatile temper. She counted to ten under her breath before she turned to the boy.

"So I put a lot of hours into this program, hours I didn't have to spare.'' Her eyes widened as a horrible thought struck her. "Did you do that on purpose?" she asked, her voice raising. "Did you deliberately try to destroy the templates?"

"No!"

"Really?"

"Yeah. I don't care about your stupid program."

"Well, what were you doing fooling around with it? Answer me!"

"I don't have to. I'm sick of you telling me what to do." Jason's own anger surfaced. He kicked a box out of his way and headed for the door. "I'm sick of this stupid race. I'm getting out of here."

"Oh, no, you're not." Kate planted herself in front of the door. Boy and woman glared at each other for a long moment. Kate took a long breath and reminded herself that she was supposed to be the adult here.

"Look, Jason, I'm sorry I snapped at you. Really. Can we try again? Please?"

Some of the mutinous expression left the boy's face, but he remained standing stiff and still before her.

"What were you doing on the computer?" she asked in a milder tone.

"I was just seeing how it worked." Jason's lower lip stuck out, but at least he raised his head to look at her. "I've never tried one of these little jobbies before."

Kate almost missed the significance of his words. Her eyes narrowed as they studied the freckled face before her. "Have you tried other kinds of computers?"

Jason shrugged. "Some. We have a few old ones at school that I mess around on. Some company donated them. Half of them don't even work. But we're supposed to get some new ones this year."

"What do you do on them?" she asked, genuinely curious now.

The boy shrugged again. "I use the typing tutor and play a few word games. And a Magic Quest game. I'm pretty good at that."

"I've got a game like that on my computer. It's pretty tough, though. Do you want to try it after we finish cleaning up here and get some lunch?"

"I guess so."

It wasn't much, Kate told herself grimly as they straightened the office and gathered their belongings. But maybe, just maybe, it was a start.

Seven

Later that afternoon, Dan rang Kate's doorbell three times before she answered.

"Hi, beautiful." He bent to kiss her—a hard hungry kiss that left him aching and Kate panting. "Were you in your tub or something?"

"Hmm?" Kate leaned back in the circle of his strong arms to smile up at him.

"What took you so long to get to the door?" He put her gently out of his arms.

"I was being attacked by the evil sorcerer. I had to zap him with my magic cudgel to get away." She waved toward Jason, hunched over her computer, tapping on the keyboard with two flying fingers. The boy called out to her, never taking his eyes from the small, greenish screen.

"Kate, look! I figured out that if you take the mirror from the wall you can reflect the spell right back onto the bad guy. He'll destroy himself. Oh, hi, Dan."

"Hi, yourself, kid." Dan turned back to Kate, brows raised.

"Jason is a near genius at foiling dark knights and wicked sorcerers. He's faster on the keyboard with two fingers than I am with ten. And much more blood-thirsty," she added, laughing at Jason's low, exultant yell.

"Yes! Got him! Took his head right off with the sword of light."

Despite Dan's vociferous protests, he soon found himself taking Kate's seat beside the boy. She hung over his shoulder and tried to help. He grinned when Kate and Jason both laughed, then groaned every time his clumsy fingers hit the wrong key. After sending them all to the darkest dungeons for the third time, he was banished to the couch and the baseball game on TV.

Dan was more than content to relax on the comfy sofa with Rico sprawled across his lap in blissful companionship. He kept a lazy eye on the TV, but Kate's burnished hair and Jason's excited shouts captured his attention more than the players' lackluster performance. His gut tightened slowly as he surveyed the jean-clad woman, sitting with her back to him and her head bent close to Jason's. Her fluffy pink top followed the long curve of her back and flared over the swelling hips. A vivid memory of planting kisses all along those hips and back flashed through his mind. Dan took a hasty swallow of his beer and shifted on the couch. Suddenly he couldn't seem to find a comfortable position. Rico lifted his head when his pillow moved for the fifth time in as many minutes and sent Dan a reproachful look.

"Sorry, boy," Dan told him quietly. His gaze went back to Kate.

Just how much space did one woman need, anyway? He'd been more patient than he ever believed he could be with anyone, especially a feisty, hot-tempered female who fired his blood with her laughter and his imagination with her long-limbed body.

At first, his restraint had made him feel almost virtuous, like some medieval knight waiting for his lady to bestow her favors. That feeling faded completely the day of their visit to Petroglyph Park. When he'd put Kate, all soft and pliant, out of his arms and seen frustration deepen her eyes to a bluish purple, he knew he wasn't cut out for the role of noble knight. All this week his own frustration had grown. Hot, edgy, irritable, mounting frustration. Enough was enough.

He was more of a cowboy than a knight, Dan decided. And not one of the good guys in a white hat, either. He'd be damned if he was going to be content with lifting his woman gently to the saddle and riding off into the sunset. Kate would be lucky if she made it to dusk before he threw her across his shoulder and carried her off to his bed. And if she brought up any more objections or mentioned her blasted schedule once more, he might just handcuff her to the damn bed frame. His groin tightened as he planned the evening to come. The ball game drew to a tepid finish, the dark sorcerer was finally vanquished and Dan's patience ran out.

"Come on, you two. It's after four. Let's get some hamburgers, then take Jason home." He pushed a protesting Rico out of his lap and rose.

"That's the first time he's even said goodbye," Kate mused, watching Jason make his way toward the battered screen door of his house.

"I was amazed to find you two actually talking to each other this afternoon," Dan commented as he backed the car out of the driveway.

"Well, it was touch and go for a while. I lost my cool with him this morning and we had a little shouting match. I'm afraid I'm not very good with kids."

Dan reached over to take her hand. "You're doing fine. Just give him some time and attention. That's what he needs most."

"You have such natural instincts with him," Kate mused, twining her fingers in his. "He responds to you so well. Didn't you want children of your own?"

He lifted his shoulders in a slight shrug. "I did. My ex-wife didn't."

Kate glanced from his impassive face to the hand holding hers. His fingers had tightened imperceptibly, unconsciously. She felt their painful bite, and a corresponding pain clutched at her heart. Dan had never known a family's love, as a child or as a man.

Kate was quiet for the rest of the trip. She roused only when he pulled into an unfamiliar parking lot.

"My place," he responded to her unspoken question.

Nodding, she followed him up the stairs. A smile spread across her face as she surveyed this man's kingdom. It reflected his personality. Two large, comfortable sofas in soft leather faced each other with a large glass coffee table between them. Books, some open and laid facedown, some stacked haphazardly, littered the coffee table and spilled over onto the end tables. Shelves filled with more books and an expensive-looking stereo system stretched the length of one wall. At the far end of the living room, sliding glass doors led to a small balcony with a view across the valley to the west mesa.

Kate could see the five volcanoes sketched across the far horizon in slowly darkening purple majesty.

Dan went into the small kitchenette, to return a few minutes later with a beer for him, a glass of wine for her. He grinned in response to her appreciative sip.

"I figure I can invest in some good wine if you'll invest in some decent coffee. I like it strong and black in the mornings."

Kate looked at him over the rim of her glass as he settled himself beside her on the couch. She took another sip and savored the sharp, fruity tang while she considered his words.

"Do you think it's time for me to start making you coffee in the mornings?" she asked him slowly.

"Nope." Dan smiled. "I'll make it. You may not be ready, Kate, but I am. More than ready. I can't play the gentleman anymore and leave you at your doorstep with a chaste kiss while you try to find a way to fit me into your nice, neat, well-planned world. I'll just fit you into mine, instead."

He set his beer down on the coffee table and reached for her glass. Kate watched his hands move from the drinks to her arms. He pulled her against his chest and settled his chin on top of her head. He felt so good—so strong and solid and good. She wrapped her arms around his ribs and fit herself against him.

"That's better. You need to relax more. You worry too much."

"I can't help it," Kate murmured, nestling her cheek against his warmth. "I have to know where I'm going, try to anticipate and plan for what's coming next."

"I'll tell you where you're going." His voice rumbled against her ear. "You're going into my bedroom.

And there's no way you can plan for what's coming next.''

When Dan lifted her in his arms and headed down the dim hallway, Kate smiled to herself. Funny that they both decided to end their self-imposed restraint at the same time. After her long, sleepless night, filled with chaotic, yearning thoughts of Dan, she still hadn't resolved just where this relationship was going. But Kate had finally acknowledged, deep in her heart, that wherever it went, she hoped they would be together.

Still, when he laid her on his bed she bit her lip as she looked up at the face hovering over her. She sensed a new determination in him and felt the faint flutter of walls closing in on her.

''Don't worry so.'' Dan's fingers worked at the zipper of her jeans. ''You don't have to have a preplanned milestone chart for everything in your life. Just lie back and enjoy it.''

Kate gave a shaky laugh when Dan wiggled his eyebrows and gave her an exaggerated, lecherous grin. Her last conscious thought, before his hands and mouth went to work on her, was that she'd do just that—enjoy it.

And she did. Dan stretched every stroke and every kiss to their limit. He lingered over her breasts and belly and the insides of her thighs until she felt tiny, rippling sensations over every square inch of her body. When she brought a hand down to give him back stroke for stroke, he raised it over her head, capturing both her wrists in one big fist.

''Oh, no, Katey mine. I don't want you doing any work of any kind tonight. Tonight, I'm going to show you that *not* being in control can have its own rewards.''

Kate squirmed under him, half aroused, half embarrassed at the pleasure her own helplessness gave her. Dan didn't even release her hands to remove her loose top. He just pushed it up until his free hand and his mouth had access to her aching nipples. In the same manner, he dragged her jeans and panties down until he could free one of her legs, then left the clothes tangled around the other. Kate gasped when his knee pushed itself between hers and forced them apart, leaving her open and vulnerable.

Even when he fumbled with the zipper on his own jeans, he held her. When he used his teeth and one hand on the foil packet he pulled out of his pocket, he held her.

"This might take a little practice," he muttered when he dropped the package on her chest for the second time.

"Dan, for heaven's sakes, let me loose. Let me touch you."

"Nope. This is my fantasy. I kinda like being the one with the black hat, after all."

"What in the world are you talking about?" she asked breathlessly. His hand had finished its business and was now buried in the curls between her wide-spread legs.

"Never mind."

He bent his head to her breast. Kate felt the sharp edge of his teeth against her engorged nipple the same moment he slid his fingers into her core. Her body arched, pulling against his restraining hand and the heavy leg thrown over hers. She couldn't escape him. He filled every one of her senses. She felt the rasp of his mustache against the tender skin of her breast. She breathed in the scent of him, dark and musky and all male.

When he thrust into her, Kate thought she would explode. Dan wouldn't allow her even that release. He pulled out slowly, letting her feel every ridge and rock-hard inch. He held himself just outside her until her rioting senses stopped whirling. Then he thrust in again, so hard and deep she almost screamed in wild pleasure. Her hips bucked against his and he moved against her, fast and hard.

Kate's consciousness narrowed, her senses sharpened. Dan released her wrists to cradle her head, holding her steady for his kiss. Her hands finally free, Kate clutched the sleek sinews that flexed with every thrust. She panted, straining against him, clenching and unclenching her muscles around his shaft. A rushing tide of heat began at her core, spread slowly, then moved with gathering momentum up her body. Groaning far back in her throat, Kate climaxed in a blinding rush of sensation.

Vaguely, Kate heard Dan give a low, savage moan. He stiffened, holding himself rigid while she rode the waves of pleasure. When the world stopped spinning, she opened her eyes to find him watching her intently.

"That was almost worth it," he told her with grim satisfaction.

Kate swallowed, feeling a rawness in her throat. "What? What was worth what?"

"Seeing you explode in my arms is almost worth the weeks we've wasted. You've just run out of space, woman."

Before Kate could gather her disordered thoughts enough for a coherent response, Dan began to move again. Slowly at first, then with gathering force.

* * *

Dan left on Tuesday for a conference in California, something to do with the migration of gangs from the West Coast. Kate felt his absence more with each passing day. Memories of their nights together would crop up at the most embarrassing moments—like when one of her engineers brought up the milestone chart for the first series test pattern for the integrated system. Kate stared at the computer screen with unseeing eyes. She could hear Dan's deep voice telling her that life didn't have to be laid out in precise, measured increments just before he made her forget where she was, much less where she was going.

"With luck, we can run the first pattern this weekend."

She blinked up at the engineer hovering over her shoulder. "Oh...great, Rich."

She shook away the last of her preoccupation and bent over the screen. "We just might make up for the days we lost trying to work out the bugs in that faulty unit."

She felt a familiar excitement course through her as she went back to her own workstation and called up the timelines. While she waited for the program to come up, she glanced at the calendar hanging on the wall of her workstation. They could just do it. With luck and a lot of late nights, they could still finish a week ahead of schedule, just enough to qualify for the bonus. It would mean working day and night for the next few weeks. This was the most critical phase of the whole integration effort.

Kate knew taking down the lab's other supercomputer was a significant undertaking with global ramifications. Phillips Lab was one of four existing nodes for air force scientific research, heavily involved in the space program. When she first started the contract, an earnest young air force major had gone into excruciating detail on the lab's role in space research. Even keeping to an unclassified level of detail, he'd lost Kate after the first five minutes. All she knew was that if she delayed his supercomputing time beyond the period scheduled for it to be down, the fate of the world would be in jeopardy.

Her adrenaline was still pumping when she left late that night. It wasn't until she was halfway home that she remembered she was supposed to pick up Jason the next morning. No, she wasn't picking him up this time. His foster mother was going to drop him off at the medical center because she had some appointment, Kate recalled. It was after midnight now. Too late to call and cancel. She'd have to try to catch them before they left in the morning.

She smiled as she drove through the darkness, feeling a sense of forward movement, of definable progress. Jason was at least talking to her, the job was going well and Dan . . . well, Dan was filling her mind and her nights more and more. She'd been both surprised and a little alarmed by how much she missed him this past week. She let herself into the house and fell asleep thinking of various ways to welcome him home.

Exhausted, she slept through the alarm the following morning. It was after eight when she woke to see the sunlight streaming through the skylights in her bedroom. Kate yelped and scrambled up, dislodging a snoring Rico from his nest at the foot of the bed. She rushed through her shower and pulled on a pair of slacks and a light jersey top. She hated being late. It threw off her schedule for the whole day and made her feel as though she never quite caught up. While she waited impatiently for the coffee to perk, she punched Jason's home number into the phone. Getting no answer, she tried the number at the outer office of the medical center. The phone rang half a dozen times before she heard a hesitant hello.

"Jason? I'm sorry I didn't catch you before you left your house. Look, I've got to go in to work for a little while this morning. Can you keep busy until I get there?"

"Yeah, I guess so."

"There should be a stack of new race-entry applications. Why don't you open and sort through them? I'll be there as soon as I can, okay?"

"Okay."

"Is Dr. Chavez there yet? Can you put him on the line?"

She spoke to him and explained that she had to work and that she'd be there as soon as she could. He agreed to check on Jason occasionally. It would only be for a few hours, she told herself as she rushed out to the garage.

Kate kept one harried eye on the clock throughout the long, frantic morning. The first test pattern bombed and they had to restart it. Around noon, she called Jason again. He sounded bored and irritable when he finally picked up the phone.

"I can't get away after all, Jason. Do you think your foster mother could come get you?"

She frowned at the brief silence that filled the phone. Her conscience pricked her. Despite the urgency of the work, she could halt the test program and slip out for the hour it would take to drive across town and back.

"I'll get a ride."

Kate felt a guilty stab of relief at Jason's concurrence. "The center's only a few miles from your house. I'll call Mrs. Grant. If she can't come for you, I will."

Sue Grant was less than enthusiastic about gathering up her other children to go get Jason. Kate wished she hadn't even called, but the other woman snapped that she'd go and cut the connection. Kate hung up, biting her lower lip, and tried to shrug off her nagging guilt. She'd make it up to the boy, she promised. Next week they'd do something special. She turned back to her console to lose herself in the test pattern once again.

"Where is she?"

Kate jumped at the deep, angry voice slicing through the quiet of the lab. She looked up to find Trish holding open the heavy doors, Dan looming just beyond her.

The two men sitting beside her scooted back their wheeled chairs when she jumped up and headed for the entrance.

"Dan! I thought you weren't coming back until tomorrow. What are you doing here?"

Kate's wide, welcoming smile faltered at the rigid set to his face. His black brows were drawn together in a dark slash across his forehead.

"Come out here."

Kate stared, totally confused by his harsh tone and cold look. She'd never seen him angry before, but there was no mistaking the fury in his eyes. She walked out into the corridor and pulled the heavy door shut on Trish's interested gaze.

"Come on." Dan didn't wait for the door to close behind her before he took her arm in a hard grip. He turned and headed down the dim corridor, pulling her behind him.

"Hey, wait a minute. Dan, stop!" Kate stumbled, trying to keep up with his rapid stride. She jerked her arm free, almost as angry as she was confused now. "Just what do you think you're doing?"

She almost tripped over her own feet when Dan whirled to face her. "I'm taking you to the hospital. So you can visit your charge."

Kate backed away from the icy rage shimmering in his eyes. "What...what charge?" she whispered. "Oh, God, you don't mean Jason?"

"Right the first time, lady," Dan told her, his voice as cold and as hard as his eyes.

"What happened? Is he all right?"

"No."

The stark word hit Kate like a fist in the stomach. She lifted a trembling hand to her lips.

"He's in intensive care."

"Intensive care?" Kate's voice cracked.

"Yeah. I guess he got a little bored waiting for you at the medical center and took off on his own. The police have been looking for him ever since Mrs. Grant reported him missing late this evening. They just found him an hour ago."

Dan took her arm again. "In an alley. Unconscious."

Eight

Kate never knew the hours between midnight and dawn could stretch so endlessly. Nor had she realized how many violent emotions could wrack a person at one time. She stood in front of the window of the lounge in St. Joseph's Hospital, arms wrapped tight around her chest. Her unseeing eyes gazed at the few city lights still glowing in the empty hours before sunrise.

Dan's credentials had gained her a brief visit with Jason. The few minutes she'd spent staring down at his still body had helped neither him nor her. The boy was still unconscious, with a severe concussion. He looked so young and helpless in the wide bed, with tubes and IVs snaking from his body. A vicious bruise discolored one cheek and he had grotesque circles around both his eyes. Thick bandages covered one side of his head, where a "blunt instrument" had slammed up against his skull. They still weren't quite sure what had caused the injury. Neither the patrolmen nor the paramedics had found anything in the alley that looked like a weapon.

The lights outside the window blurred as tears filled her eyes. Emotions roiled through her—guilt, fear, a nagging sense of failure, desperate hope that Jason would recover. When she tried to focus on one feeling, another would rise up to swamp her. She couldn't ever remember being so confused, or so helpless.

For the first time in her adult life she found herself questioning her values. Since her very first afterschool job, she'd believed that hard work and a little talent would get her everything she wanted: financial security, a nice home, challenging work. And maybe a family someday, when she'd met all her other goals. Now she faced the bitter fact that she'd put so much emphasis on her job, on getting ahead, on sticking to her damned schedule, that it could have cost a child's life.

With wrenching uncertainty, Kate wondered if she would ever have children. How could any parent bear the pain of seeing their child lying so pale and still, stretched out in a wide hospital bed? Her stomach clenched again.

"Here, Kate, have some coffee."

She took the cup Dan offered and blinked back incipient tears, unable to speak through the tight constriction of her throat. Although his anger at her had dissipated, Kate still had difficulty facing him.

"And a couple of sweet rolls from the vending machine."

She shook her head, not trusting her voice.

"Go ahead. You need the energy. This could be a long night."

"I'm not hungry," she managed to whisper.

"Well, I am," Dan replied, tearing open the cellophane wrapper. "I didn't have anything on the plane tonight."

Kate frowned, remembering what she'd forgotten in her fear and panic over Jason. "Why did you come back early? I thought you had a meeting with some other police officials tomorrow, after the convention."

"I worked it in earlier." Dan gave her a long, slow look from under half-lowered lids. "I wanted to get home, to you."

Thick waves of guilt washed over her when she remembered how she'd been looking forward with delicious anticipation to welcoming him back. She'd even bought a sexy little teddy, with ribbons that conveniently tied at the shoulder. She'd imagined in excruciating detail just how he'd untie the ribbons. Those frivolous, silly plans seemed obscene against the stark reality of Jason lying in a hospital bed. She swallowed fiercely, forcing tears back.

"Why didn't you call when you got in?" she asked.

"I did. There was no answer at your place, so I figured you were at work. I decided to stop by my office on the way home from the airport. Detective Alvarado heard about Jason and told me."

Dan took a sip of his coffee before continuing. "I got to the trauma center just after they brought him in. When he was stabilized and moved to ICU, I came for you."

Kate groaned, leaning her head back against the wall. "I'll never forgive myself for leaving him alone this morning, never!"

He looked at her steadily, sympathy in his eyes. "That's something you'll have to work through for yourself, Kate. I can't help you. I can only be here for you.''

Dan's quiet words dropped like stones in the echoing well of her heart. Kate wanted to look away again, to avoid his steady, level look, but she wouldn't allow herself that small act of cowardice.

"Tell me what happened. Jason was fine when I talked to him at noon, and his foster mother was on her way to pick him up.''

"He called her back to say he had a ride home and he'd see her later. She didn't start to get nervous until late afternoon. She finally notified the police early this evening.''

"I wish she'd called me. I could have gone to look for him.''

"She did. Several times. She only had your home phone number.''

Dan's voice held no accusation, but Kate flinched. She took a deep breath, pushing her guilt down. Remorse and recriminations would come later, when she could berate herself in private. Right now she needed to focus on Jason.

"Do you have any idea who might have hurt him or why?''

Dan shook his head. "No. We'll have to wait and see what he says.''

"My God, he's only a boy. Who could hurt a child like that?'' Kate cried.

"There aren't any children on the street. Only losers and a few who think they've won. I can name a hundred hurting souls who might try to relieve their pain by inflicting it on others.''

Kate stared at the man opposite her, hearing echoes of his own childhood in his quiet words. The minutes ticked away slowly as they sat, surrounded by the heavy stillness that descends just before dawn. A few yards away, medical personnel worked and talked in low voices at the ICU control station. Orderlies moved along the dimmed hallways, pushing rubber-wheeled carts.

Faint red streaks were just piercing the darkness of the night when the physician on duty came to look for Dan. Kate watched, shoulders hunched with tension, while the two men conferred quietly. She breathed a ragged sob at Dan's tired but relieved smile as he came back to her.

"Jason's going to be okay. He woke up for a few moments and knew his name, understood where he was. The doctor's confident he hasn't suffered any permanent damage."

Kate bit her lip to hold back her tears. She nodded when he told her quietly it was time to go home. They walked out of the hospital into the graying half-light of morning and headed for Dan's car.

"What will happen to him now?" Kate asked, her eyes on the slowly lightening street outside the window. In the window's reflection, she saw Dan give her a long look. Slowly she turned to face him.

"The Grants have washed their hands of him. Mrs. Grant told the caseworker tonight he was too much trouble and she wouldn't have him back in her home. She has other foster children to worry about."

Kate felt a knife twist in her chest. Not only had she abandoned the boy, but as a result of her actions, he'd lost the only home he had.

"So where will he go, once he gets out of the hospital?"

"His caseworker will try to line up a new foster home and convince the judge to allow another placement." Dan glanced over at her. Even in the dim light, Kate could see the doubt and regret in his eyes.

"It'll be tough finding a family who'll want to take him in, with his record of running away and the break-ins. I'm afraid Jason's facing the county home."

"No! We can't just give up on him so easily."

Dan's brows raised slightly and he slanted her another, deliberate look.

Kate flushed. "*I* can't give up on him. I made a mistake and I'm not about to let Jason suffer for it for the rest of his life."

A surge of determination swept through her, blunting the sharp edges of pain.

"What do you think you can do?"

"I...I don't know yet," Kate admitted. "I'll have to talk to the caseworker. And to Jason, when he's able."

That would be the hardest part, Kate knew. But she had to try. She couldn't just shrug her shoulders and walk off, leaving the boy to face the consequences of her negligence.

She was still weighing her limited options when Dan brought her back to the lab to get her car, then followed her home. The golden dawn backlit the mountains behind her house as she swung into her driveway. Dan stopped her with a gentle hand on her arm when she would have led the way into the house.

"'Night, Kate." Dan leaned down to brush her lips lightly.

"Aren't you coming in?"

"No, I'm tired." He ran his knuckle down her cheek in soft, gentle strokes. "We both need some rest."

Kate bit her lip. What she needed was the feel of Dan's arms around her and his deep, soothing voice telling her everything would be all right. But everything was not all right, she reminded herself, and he looked even more exhausted than she felt. She nodded slowly.

"When will I see you?"

Dan smiled, the lines at the corners of his eyes crinkling. "Later. Get some sleep." He turned her around, gave her rear a gentle shove and pushed her toward Rico's ecstatic, wiggling body.

Kate closed the door and knelt down to take the grinning, slurping dog into her arms. Not for the first time, she understood why some people filled their homes and their lives with pets. Those eccentric old maids with all their cats and dogs weren't so dotty after all, she realized. Rico's warm, wet, uncritical love was incredibly soothing to her lacerated soul. She fell asleep, the dog draped across her feet at the bottom of the bed, just as the sun cleared the first mountain peak.

The next few days were as emotionally trying as she'd feared. She only saw Dan once, but he was distracted and only had time for a quick sandwich in a crowded coffee shop. She made two trips downtown to see Jason's caseworker, who was having little luck finding another foster home. At least the doctor was cheerful, assuring her the boy had suffered no permanent damage and predicting his complete recovery within a week.

She went daily to see Jason in the room he shared with two other boys. He shrugged off her halting apologies and kept his bruised face turned to the window during most of her visits, giving no sign that he was pleased or that he even cared whether she came to see him. He wouldn't talk about what happened—not to her or to Dan or to his caseworker. He'd hardly talk at all.

Kate refused to give up. She ignored his closed expression and drew up a chair beside his bed to fill him in on the growing numbers of race entrants, Rico's latest antics and even, in desperation, her mother's frequent calls to inquire about his progress.

Nothing seemed to penetrate, however, until she stopped by after work one night. As she was getting out of her car, her eyes fell on the little laptop computer in the passenger seat. Thoughtfully, she eyed the gray plastic case. It worked once, it might work again, she thought grimly.

She plunked the computer down on the tray beside Jason's bed and plugged it in. After some coaxing, she got him and the other boys in the room into a bloodthirsty quest to retrieve an abducted galactic princess. For the first time, Jason's battered face lost some of its tightness as he became immersed in the game.

"Here, keep this with you," Kate told him at the end of visiting hours. She closed the case and stored the little computer in the stand beside his bed.

"Aren't you afraid it'll get stolen?" Jason asked, with unconscious irony.

"No," Kate told him, smiling. "And I expect you to have Princess Tessala back and the whole crew off on the next level of adventure when I come tomorrow."

"You don't have to come every day." Jason picked at the blue cord cover, not meeting her eyes.

"Do you want me to?"

The boy shrugged, head still bent.

"Then I'll come," Kate told him. She gathered her purse and headed for the door. "'Night, Jason."

"'Night, Kate."

She almost missed his muttered goodbye. She turned back, but the boy was already settled down under the covers, his shoulder hunched away from her. Kate stood for a moment in the door, staring at the pitifully small mound he made in the wide bed. Her jaw clenched. She'd be damned if she would allow the bureaucracy to send this boy to an institution. She fumbled in her purse for her calling card and headed for a phone.

Three days later Dan sat beside an agitated Kate in the cavernous, upstairs airport lounge. He watched her fidget with her purse strap while a throng of arriving and departing travelers flowed around them.

"Are you sure you can handle this, Kate?"

"No, I'm not sure, but I'm going to give it one helluva try."

Dan felt his heart lurch. This was the Kate he loved, this fierce, determined creature. In the last couple days he'd worked through his disappointment in her for leaving Jason alone, just as she had worked through her own guilt and bleak despair. Everyone made mistakes. He'd certainly made his share. But Kate was going to do something about hers. She'd detailed her plan in a breathless phone call only this morning, asking—no demanding his support.

With characteristic stubbornness, she'd bullied Judge Chavez into a special hearing this afternoon, in just a few hours. Now she waited with unconcealed impatience for the next piece to fall in place. Dan bit back a grin, wondering if she'd programmed the whole damn scheme, complete with milestones and color-coded objectives, into her computer.

"I hope the plane isn't late," she said, worrying. "The judge wasn't too thrilled with making a special trip in this afternoon."

She stood and began to pace back and forth, in short, restless steps. "Are you sure Detective Alvarado will get Jason there?"

"Yes, I'm sure."

"I just hope the caseworker gets the time of the hearing right. I left two messages on her recorder."

"She'll be there."

"Dr. Henderson assured me he could slip out for—"

Dan reached out a lazy hand and pulled her down beside him. "The doc will be there. Calm down, Kate. You're making me nervous with all that pacing."

When she smiled at him, Dan felt a tight knot begin to unravel in his gut. He hadn't seen her smile in days, nor had he realized how much he'd missed it.

"If that's nervous, I'd hate to see you relaxed. You'd probably slide to the floor in one huge, boneless blob."

"I'm saving my energy for—"

"There she is!"

Kate jumped up and ran toward a group of passengers just passing through the control point. Dan watched her throw her arms around a small, high-cheeked woman whose fading red hair still bore traces of her daughter's bright mahogany. The two women hugged and kissed and stood chattering while waves of passengers eddied around them. Dan waited patiently until Kate clutched her mother's arm and tugged her over to him. The older woman lifted one brow as she took his measure, then dismissed his courteous "Mrs. O'Sullivan" with a wave of her hand.

"Call me Mary Catherine. We might as well start as we mean to go on. From what my Kathleen *hasn't* told me in her calls these last few weeks, I'd bet my grandmother's prayer book you're well beyond the formal stage by now.''

Dan laughed at Kate's smothered groan. "Good enough, Mary Catherine. And you're right, we're well beyond formal. We've passed downright informal, in fact."

"Oh, for Pete's sake, come on, you two. You can discuss the precise stage of our...relationship later." Kate herded them both toward the escalator. "We have to claim mother's luggage and get her some lunch before the hearing."

Dan dutifully retrieved Mary Catherine's bags, then settled the women in the airport's lavish restaurant.

"I really appreciate your coming so quickly, Mother." Kate barely got the words out around a mouth full of warm sopapilla slathered in honey. Dan handed her another napkin as she licked the sticky goo off her fingers.

"It's not as if I had other, unbreakable commitments, dear." Mary Catherine picked up one corner of the huge, puffed pastry and stared at it doubtfully.

"Go ahead, they're wonderful," Kate told her, swallowing the last chewy chunk. She reached for her glass of ice tea, then stopped, a slight frown marring the line of her brow. "I thought you were busy with your volunteer work and church activities. And at the senior center."

The older woman shrugged, taking tentative bites of the sopapilla.

Kate's frown deepened. "You're living in one of the best-run retirement centers in California. They pride themselves on all their activities, from golf to chess tournaments to Jazzercise."

Mary Catherine gave up on the dough square and set it carefully on her half-full plate. "Those are just time fillers, darling. Not quite like working full-time and cooking and keeping my own house."

The older woman's eyes, so like her daughter's in color, twinkled as she turned to Dan. "Kate bought me this beautiful condominium and insisted I retire when she got her first promotion. I tried to get her to spend the bonus on herself, but she had her list of 'to-do's' all laid out and I was at the top of the list."

Dan laughed. "I'm familiar with your daughter's determination to proceed according to plan. She's got a master schedule for the next twenty years."

"And I'll bet you're throwing her schemes all out of kilter, aren't you?"

Mary Catherine grinned at Dan, and they both turned to the subject of their conversation, sitting between them in frowning silence. Dan could see confusion, and a hint of hurt, clouding Kate's expressive eyes.

"I thought you were happy there, Mother. I . . . I thought you'd be thrilled to leave your twenty-hour days behind and enjoy life a little."

"I am, darling, I am." Her mother reached over to pat her hand. "But it's good to be needed. It's good to have *you* need me again. That's why I was so quick to jump on a plane when you called. Now tell me about this boy, Jason."

Dan watched Kate struggle to throw off the doubt still lingering on her face. He sat back, only half listening while she recounted the boy's history. Obviously, her mother's comments bothered her. Dan wondered if she was beginning to realize that even the best-laid plans were fallible. That not everyone lived their life according to a preplanned agenda.

* * *

Less than an hour later, they walked up the steps to the county courthouse. Dan stayed in the background when they entered the judge's chambers, where the informal hearing would be held. While waiting for the judge's arrival, Kate introduced her mother to Jason and his caseworker. Dan could see the doubt and fear and a pitiful hope in the boy's blue eyes as he looked up at the two women. They all rose as Judge Chavez entered.

"Ms. O'Sullivan, you've petitioned the court for temporary custody of Jason Stone. Do you really understand the magnitude of the responsibility you're requesting?"

Kate stood and met the judge's hard look with a characteristic tilt to her chin. "Probably not. I've not been responsible for anyone but myself for years, until I agreed to sponsor Jason. And I didn't do a very good job at that."

She took a deep breath. "Judge Chavez, I know you don't have much reason to trust me after I let Jason down, but I assure you it won't happen again. I want to rectify my mistake."

"I hope you're not toying with a child's life just to assuage some misplaced sense of guilt, Ms. O'Sullivan."

Kate stiffened at the sharp tone. "No, ma'am. I'm not using Jason to excuse my negligence. But since my actions did contribute directly to his problems, I want to help solve them."

"Temporary custody won't solve his difficulties."

"It will buy him some time to recover completely and be placed in another, hopefully more supportive, foster home."

"What makes you think you're qualified to see to a child's needs?" Julia Chavez pushed her glasses up on her nose and leaned forward, her gaze sharp and stern.

"I'm not. But my mother flew in from California this morning and will stay with us for the duration. She's more than qualified, as I can personally attest."

Mary Catherine O'Sullivan stood beside her daughter. Viewing them from behind, Dan saw identical stiff spines and an almost palpable aura of determination radiating from them both.

Judge Chavez studied them both for a long moment, then turned to the boy.

"What about you, Jason? I saw from your case-worker's report you still won't tell us what happened to cause your hospitalization. What assurance do I have that you won't abuse Ms. O'Sullivan's hospitality or run away again?"

Jason swallowed. "I won't."

"How can I believe that? You ran away from the Grants, twice."

The boy's face paled, making his fading bruises stand out in stark relief. He struggled for words, but could only manage, "I won't."

"Will you tell us what happened? Who hurt you?"

Kate bit her lip so hard she tasted the faint, metallic tincture of blood. With determined obstinacy, Jason had refused to discuss the incident. She was afraid the judge would hold his stubborn silence against him.

"Please, Judge Chavez, the doctor has submitted a private opinion on Jason's injuries." Kate leaned forward in her eagerness. "He thinks—"

"I've read the report, Ms. O'Sullivan."

Dan lifted one hand to stroke his mustache. He'd talked with Judge Chavez himself earlier, voicing his own opinion of what might have happened. He and the doctor believed the boy had somehow run afoul of his old gang. The hematoma was severe, but not as severe as if he'd been attacked by an adult intending serious harm.

"The juvenile probation officer has also submitted a report," Kate offered.

The woman behind the broad wooden desk gave a faint smile at Kate's determined persistence. "I've read that, also, Ms. O'Sullivan." She sat back in her high leather chair and surveyed the assembled group.

"Obviously, you're all sincere in wanting to help Jason." She leveled a steady look at Kate, still standing beside her mother. "My head tells me you don't really grasp the difficulties associated with taking a child into your home, but my heart says you've already learned one very valuable lesson the hard way. Children demand time and attention. Can you spare time from your work and your other interests?"

Julia Chavez's dry tone and bland glance at Dan weren't lost on anyone in the room. Mary Catherine's brows rose as she looked at her daughter's flushed face, and Dan knew they'd have some explaining to do later.

"Yes, ma'am," Kate managed through stiff lips.

"All right," the judge said briskly, coming to a decision. "I'll ask Welfare to expedite your background check and psychological profile. Assuming the reports are positive, you'll have temporary custody for sixty days. You'll report to the caseworker weekly, and continue your community-service program."

Kate hurried over to Jason as the judge rose and gathered her papers. From the back of the room, Dan watched as she held out her hand and, after a moment's hesitation, Jason slipped his into hers.

Julia Chavez turned back. "Incidentally, my husband tells me you and Jason have done yeoman work on the race. He couldn't have managed without you both."

Kate and Jason shared a wide smile. Dan strolled forward, took Mary Catherine's arm and escorted her across the room. "Come on, troops. I think this calls for a celebration. How about hot dogs and hamburgers at your place?"

"Some celebration," Kate laughed.

"I like hot dogs," Jason volunteered shyly. "With chili."

"And onions," Mary Catherine added, taking his other hand.

"Dripping with mustard and relish." Dan smacked his lips.

"Yech!" Kate looked at the circle of grinning faces and relented. "All right, all right, hot dogs it is. If there are any left. Rico likes them, too, you know." With that parting shot, she led the way home.

"You cook a mean chili dog, woman."

Kate sighed contentedly and snuggled down into Dan's arms as best she could on the rattan patio lounge. Although roomy and comfortably padded, it wasn't made for two people, let alone two generously sized people.

"They were pretty good, weren't they? Not that I can claim full credit."

In fact, she'd barely been allowed in the kitchen. Dan had decided to instruct a still-shy Jason in the fine art of grilling hot dogs over the Jenn-Air. Kate and her mother had been relegated to onion chopping and chili-cooking duty. Kate had stepped in to save the last half-dozen wieners after Dan "accidentally" dropped two to the ever-alert Rico and Jason had burnt his to blackened cinders. Just the way he liked them, he solemnly declared.

Kate turned her head on Dan's shoulder, listening to the faint call of coyotes sounding a distant counterpoint to the soft, lilting sounds of Mary Catherine's favorite tape of Irish ballads. They'd taken Jason back to the hospital. He'd move in with Kate within the next few days, according to Judge Chavez. Her mother had excused herself for the night, claiming a need to unpack. Kate and Dan had retired to the patio for the first private moment in days. If being poked in the back every few minutes by a large, wet nose could be called private, Kate amended, pushing Rico away once more. She propped herself up on one arm to survey the complacent male beside her.

"I almost cried when Jason smiled at me tonight. Did you see him wince? It hurt his bruised face just to smile."

"It'll take time for him to recover from his hurts, both inside and out. Don't expect too much, Kate." Dan tightened his arms, drawing her close. "Don't do too much, either. For Jason, I mean."

"Why not? He deserves some care and attention. I owe it to him."

Dan curled a finger under Kate's chin, tilting her head up until she could see the moonlight tinting his eyes to silvery gray.

"You'll only hurt him more if you get too close to him. This is a temporary arrangement, remember? Don't spoil or lavish too much love on a boy who'll be going to another foster home when you leave. If he's lucky."

Kate sighed and nodded. "I know you're right, but I hate this uncertainty about Jason's future. I'm going to make sure he's happily settled before I leave."

Her voice trailed off. The thought of her leaving hung between them, like a shadow. Hesitantly, Kate looked up at Dan's face. The moonlight highlighted its lean planes and angles and glinted in his eyes.

Kate knew now she loved that face, and the man that went with it. Although she wasn't sure when in the past weeks she'd fallen for him. Maybe it was when he'd fed her and Jason pizza in the sun-drenched park. Or when he'd tumbled her into bed with laughing eagerness. But when he'd taken her hand that night at the hospital and shared her pain and fear for Jason, he'd become part of her somehow.

Slowly, her eyes drinking in the stark lines of his face, Kate lifted one finger to trace the line of his chin, then test the thick softness of his mustache. Her finger brushed back and forth gently, tentatively, only to still in startled surprise.

The high, pure tones of a tenor drifted out across the still air, filling the night with the hauntingly beautiful strains of "Danny Boy."

Kate's finger left Dan's mustache to trail slowly down his throat. She stroked the strong column, feeling his pulse beating sure and steady. Lowering her head, she placed her lips against the pulse, drinking in his blood's rhythm. She opened her lips and licked the warm skin, savoring his taste.

Above her, Dan gave a low groan and tightened his arms. The rattan creaked ominously as he pulled her up until her lips brushed his own.

" 'Oh, Danny boy, I love you so.' " Kate's breathless whisper kept time with the tenor.

He pulled back, studying her face as if trying to decide whether she meant it.

"Kate, I—"

Whatever he was about to say was lost when a loud, mournful howl suddenly filled the night air. Both Dan and Kate jumped, nearly rolling off the lounge as Rico joined in the chorus.

Under her splayed fingertips, Kate felt the laughter rumbling in Dan's chest.

"I love you, too," he managed between chuckles.

Kate sat up, her soft, languorous mood dissolving. "Could you say that again, without laughing?"

A particularly loud, distinctly unmelodic yowl rent the air.

"No," Dan gasped. Shoulders shaking, he pushed himself off the lounge and pulled Kate to her feet. Rico's enthusiastic refrain drowned out Kate's indignant protest.

While dog and tenor soared to a dramatic finale, Dan kissed her, long and hard and thoroughly.

When he lifted his head, Kate saw with satisfaction that at least the blasted man wasn't laughing anymore. His eyes blazed with a hunger that matched her own.

"Dan, we need to..."

"Yes, Kate, we need to. But not tonight, with your mother just arrived."

"We need to talk," she ground out.

"I know, sweetheart. And we will. But not now. Not when you've got your contract hanging over you and your mother to settle and Jason to care for. And Rico to quiet."

Laughter welled up in his chest once more as the dog joined in a new ballad with unrestrained gusto.

Nine

If the pace of Kate's life was hectic before, it soon became positively whirlwind. Or maybe chaotic was the more correct description, she amended, racing to work weeks later. Impatiently, she wove through what the locals considered rush hour, but Southern Californians would deem practically deserted streets.

School had started and Kate would get up early, fix breakfast, take Jason to his old school across town, then dash to work. Mary Catherine would pick him up in the afternoons and fix dinner for them all, Dan included, whenever he or Kate weren't working late, which was more often than not.

Twice, Kate had met with Jason's caseworker, who was still trying to place the boy. Once the woman had taken him to an interview, and brought him back quiet and sullen. It seemed the prospective foster parents had been turned off by Jason's record of running away and his less-than-cooperative attitude.

Kate sighed and pulled into her parking space, hurrying across the lot to the lab. Time was running out. There were only two more weeks left on her contract, three more on the lease for the house. She had to get Jason settled and sort out her relationship with Dan. And to think she'd come to Albuquerque just a few short months ago, completely unencumbered, minus boy and mother and dog and...

"We've done it, Kate!"

Trish's excited yell greeted her as she walked into the computer center. "The last data base is up and running!"

With a surge of excitement, Kate leaned over Trish's shoulder to scan the previous night's results. They'd taken the lab's last major mainframe down the night before to migrate its data base. Sure enough, the program had run smoothly, without a single glitch. This was it, Kate thought, the last major milestone.

"We're two days ahead of schedule!" one of the engineers exclaimed.

"Let's get these runs done," Kate smiled. "As soon as we certify the results and get them reviewed by the air force, there's a big bonus in this for everyone. The rest of the work is just cleanup."

The entire team hustled for the rest of the day. In the midst of their frenetic activity, Trish called Kate to the phone.

"Kate O'Sullivan speaking."

"Katie, it's Jessica. I just got word. We're in the final round of bidders on the UCLA project!"

Kate drew in a sharp breath as she listened to her part-time office manager/secretary/personal assistant babble on. The thought of leaving Albuquerque to begin her next project should have thrown Kate into a fever of anticipation. Instead she felt an incipient panic. Events were moving too fast on the job and not fast enough in her personal life. The only time she and Dan had been together lately was when they could snatch a few hours between appointments and work and the demands of her family.

A flush stained Kate's face as she thought of their rare times together. It was amazing what that man could cram into such short periods. His lovemaking got more adventurous with every stolen moment. Kate banished the vivid images before her blush melted her makeup, mumbled a response to her assistant, and went back to work.

As a reward for their efforts, Kate sent everyone home early that afternoon. Heading for her car sometime later, Kate felt a curious sense of freedom. Where before she'd always lived for her work, now she was glad they were over the hump. The long days and nights were behind them. Now she could devote some time to herself and Jason. And to Dan!

When Kate arrived home, the house was deserted. Dan had taken Jason to a ball game and Mary Catherine was indulging her passion for bingo at one of the Indian pueblos with another aficionado she'd met at the supermarket. Only Rico remained to greet her. He padded alongside while she stripped off her clothes and headed for the hot tub, his big body stretching out in blissful slumber on the wooden deck.

To her surprise, the tub failed to work its soothing magic. Kate stirred restlessly in the warm, bubbling water, fingers tapping the slick fiberglass rim. What was the matter with her? A few months ago, she would have enjoyed the peace and serenity of the night. She would've relaxed, wine in hand, eyes on the soft evening sky, congratulating herself on being able to afford such quiet, soothing luxury. Now the house seemed too still, the luxury too sterile. Kate laid her head back against the rim, finally recognizing the problem. She was lonely.

Disgruntled, Kate climbed out of the tub and dried off. She might as well get some work done, since she couldn't seem to relax. Flipping on her computer, she forced herself to work on the UCLA proposal.

She was still at the laptop when Mary Catherine let herself in some time later. With a welcome smile, Kate turned off the computer and went to greet her mother.

"Any luck?"

"No." The older woman plopped herself down on the sofa in disgust and lifted one leg, then the other, onto the magazine-strewn coffee table. "I was only two spaces away from a thousand-dollar jackpot, too."

"Hang in there, Mother," Kate said encouragingly. She joined her mother on the couch, propping her bare feet up companionably beside Mary Catherine's sneakered ones.

"Remember when you used to get excited about winning five-dollar jackpots? Father Shaw always complained you had the devil's own luck. Maybe you'll get lucky here, too, before you leave."

Mary Catherine laughed and rested her head on the back of the sofa. "I remember. Those little jackpots were real bonanzas to us then, weren't they? I think I bought your school shoes one entire year with my bingo winnings."

Kate reached over and took her mother's hand. "You know, I never heard you complain once about how hard those times were."

"What good would it have done to complain?" Her mother smiled. "Besides, I had you to love, and your grandmother helped as much as she could."

Kate laid her head back beside her mother's and stared at the ceiling thoughtfully. "It took me a long time to forgive my father for running off and leaving you to care for both of us alone."

The older woman turned, her hair rustling against the soft fabric of the couch. "Are you sure you forgave him?"

"Yes—at least I think so. Why?"

"You work so hard, Kate. You haven't taken time in your life for anything except school and work. It's as if financial success has been your only joy in life."

"I saw what marrying young and being left to raise a child by yourself did to you, Mother. Is it so wrong to want a little financial independence? To not have to depend on any man? On anyone but myself?"

"No, of course it's not wrong. But there are more important things in life than money. I'd hoped you discovered that when you and Charles became engaged."

Kate grimaced up at the ceiling. "Charles cared even more for financial security than I did. He wanted to make sure wife number two was making plenty before he ditched wife number one."

"Well, you're better off without him," Mary Catherine declared. "Now, this one, this Dan, is a different story."

Mary Catherine straightened and a determined look filled her eyes.

"You need to hold on to this one."

"I think so, too," Kate agreed softy. "But we can't seem to get around to resolving the future."

"That's because you're enjoying the present too much! Instead of using every hour you can steal away to jump in the sack, go see a priest."

"Mother!" Kate's laughing protest didn't faze Mary Catherine.

"Don't 'Mother' me, girl! I'd be more worried if you *weren't* enjoying a man like that."

Kate sputtered with laughter while her mother returned to her favorite theme. "You're thirty-one. It's long past time you were married. I want to be a grandmother!"

"Gimme a break, Mom. There's a slight matter of juggling our careers and finding some time to work things out. Besides, he hasn't asked me."

"Well, work on him."

"I'm working, I'm working," Kate protested.

Her loving mother snorted in exasperation. "Kathleen Brigit O'Sullivan, you're not the woman I think you are if you can't get a proposal out of a man who's as nuts about you as that man is."

Dan and Jason arrived home from the ball game just as the sun dipped toward the mountain peaks. They decided to work off the pent-up energy from the game in a quick run while Kate and Mary Catherine ordered pizza.

Kate smiled as they walked out on the patio, Jason in the baggy sweats she'd bought him, Dan in the disreputable cutoffs he now kept at her house. While Kate had been so wrapped up in her work, Dan had invited Jason to join him on his evening runs whenever his own work schedule would follow. To Kate's surprise, Jason had agreed. She supposed it was some kind of male bonding thing. Whatever it was, they'd fallen into a routine, jogging along the popular dirt trail that wound along the base of the mountains, an ecstatic Rico bounding ahead.

"Sure you don't want to join us?" Dan asked, one hand lifting up to brush her cheek.

"No way." Kate laughed. "Huffing and puffing and sweating along a dirt trail is not my idea of fun. I can think of a lot better things to do to my body."

"Mmm, so can I," he murmured low, for her ears only.

Kate shooed him off. "Go run. When you get back we'll have pizza. And then we need to talk."

Dan's brows rose at her determined tone.

"We finished the supercomputer integration today. The rest is just cleanup."

A satisfied gleam leapt into his eyes and he took a quick step toward her. Jason's shy voice halted him.

"That's great, Kate. Did you get the bonus?"

"Yep." She smiled. "The pizza's on me tonight. Go run, you two, and work up an appetite."

Dan drew sharp, clean air into his lungs as he set an easy pace beside Jason. The boy was running smoothly, his baggy sweats flattened against thin legs. Rico was in dog heaven, stopping frequently to sniff at interesting piles along the popular path, then charging wildly to catch up.

Dan kept his eye on his two charges, but his mind was on the talk he and Kate would have tonight. He hadn't wanted to put any more pressure on her during these past hectic weeks. She had enough strain with trying to reach Jason and working through the last, critical phase of her project. Now that she was in the home stretch at work, much of the pressure she'd been under was gone. Although Jason wasn't set yet, the caseworker had called yesterday to tell them she had a good prospect. Now was the time for Dan to make his move.

Dan dodged a delicate tumbleweed drifting across the path, thinking about Kate's success on the project, remembering her timetable. Her business was off and running. The next job had something to do with a new astronomy lab at UCLA and a batch of scientific computers. Could he ask her to give up, or at least modify, her dream for him? Could he alter the frantic pace of his job for her? Damn straight, he could.

Absently, he watched Rico's joyous pursuit of a scurrying mouse. Strange how dynamic personal relationships could be. A few weeks ago, he'd been content just to break through Kate's preoccupied focus on work and discover the sensual, passionate woman behind the computer. Now, passion wasn't enough. Now, he wanted commitment. And companionship. And love— not just sex. He wanted a future with Kate, one they'd build together. One that didn't include eighteen-hour days, seven days a week for him and six-month absences for her.

His instincts told him that's what Kate wanted, as well. He just wasn't quite sure she knew it yet. That uncertainty had held him back, kept him from asking outright for a commitment. Dan grimaced at his own gutlessness, and at the realization that his hesitancy these past weeks stemmed as much from his failed first marriage as from any nobility on his part. He didn't have a good track record at combining careers and dreams and the business of everyday life. He wanted Kate to achieve her goals, to satisfy her drive to succeed before he made his move. He wanted her to realize that he could provide her with as much pleasure in life as Phase Four or Five ever would.

But time was running out. They needed to sit down and discuss their future—calmly, rationally. He knew Kate loved him. Now he'd just have to show her that marriage was the logical next step in their relationship.

That's it, he told himself. He'd keep his zipper zipped and his mind clear. Before the night was over, he'd convince Kate they could share their dreams and their lives.

Pleased with his calm determination, Dan herded his two charges back toward the house. The sun was just sinking behind the mesa to the west, and darkness would make it difficult to run on the rock and tumbleweed-strewn path.

"Come on, guys, let's go in. The pizza's probably here. I can smell the pepperoni already."

If the pizza had arrived, they couldn't smell it when they entered the house. When Dan came through the dark kitchen, he noted the absence of any aroma, pepperoni or otherwise. Frowning, he headed for the softly lit living room. He expected to find Kate and Mary Catherine relaxing on the couch. Instead, he found Kate straining against the hold of a muscular, dark-shirted man.

Every fighting instinct, honed by years on the streets and in the marines, kicked into overdrive. In the space of a heartbeat, Dan noted the open French doors behind the twisting pair, scanned the man from head to toe for any signs of a weapon and attacked. He launched himself across the room, Rico snarling furiously at his side.

"What the—ummph!"

"Dan!"

"Grrrrrr..."

Kate's startled cry mingled with the man's grunt of pain and Rico's ferocious snarls. Dan felt a savage satisfaction when his fist connected with a midsection for the second time and the assailant went down. Planting one foot on either side of the man's body, Dan grabbed a handful of the dark shirt and pulled the intruder two feet off the carpet. He raised his fist to strike again.

All hell broke loose around him. Even to a man trained in riot-control procedures, the ensuing pandemonium was startling.

"Dan, no! Wait!"

"Heavens above, what's going on?"

"Are you crazy?"

Kate grabbed frantically at his upraised arm just as Mary Catherine came running from the back of the house. He could barely hear their shouts over Rico's furious barking. His hand tightened when the man below him scrambled backward, trying to break his hold. With a grunt, Dan heaved him to his feet.

Hauling him over to the wall, he pushed the man's face and hands up against it. He used one foot to spread his legs and ran a hand down his body to search for weapons. Rico danced around them both excitedly, his ear-splitting barks bouncing off the walls. Satisfied that the man was unarmed, Dan backed away and let him turn slowly to face the room.

"Rico, shut up!" Kate grabbed the dog's collar with one hand to haul him back.

"What's happening?" A confused, scared-looking Jason hovered at the edge of the living room.

"'That's what I'd like to know," Mary Catherine exclaimed over the dog's excited barking. She put a protective arm around the boy, hauling him close against her.

"It's all a mis—" Kate began.

"Who the hell do you think—" the man sputtered.

"Be quiet!"

Everyone in the room jumped at Dan's harsh command. Satisfied he had their attention, he moderated both his tone and the direction of his command. "Here, boy. Sit!"

"Thank heavens," Kate gasped when the barking finally stopped. She took Dan's arm again and tried to pull him away. He stepped back a few paces but kept his eyes on the man who, very prudently, remained against the wall.

"Are you okay, Kate?"

"Yes." She gulped. "Dan—"

"You sure?"

"Yes!"

He flashed her a quick look. He saw relief, exasperation and the beginnings of amusement in her eyes, but no fear.

Frowning, he turned back to the man still splayed against the wall. For the first time he noticed that the dark shirt was a well-tailored, designer edition. The blond head above the shirt was just as well tended, with a tan that deepened his angry blue eyes. His hair somehow managed to look stylish even after the manhandling.

"Who the hell are you?" Dan snapped.

"I'm Kate's fiancé. Who the hell are you?"

Dan stepped back and surveyed the man through narrowed eyes.

"I'm her lover," he drawled. "And the man she's going to marry."

A stunned silence descended over the room, to be broken long moments later by Mary Catherine's delighted chuckle.

"You did it, Kate!"

Ten

Kate barely heard her mother's gleeful exclamation. Her stunned gaze locked on the two men before her, still eyeing each other with a bristling male animosity that was totally outside her field of experience.

"What is this, Kate?" Charles accused angrily. "You didn't mention any 'lover' in our little discussion a few minutes ago."

"You...you didn't give me much of a chance to mention anything."

Kate's eyes strayed to Dan, standing with arms folded, watching her from hooded eyes. When Charles pushed himself from the wall, she forced her attention back to her indignant fiancé. Ex-fiancé!

"Well, you sure didn't waste much time in Albuquerque," he said with a sneer. "And after all I went through to start divorce proceedings! I thought you'd wait for me, Kate."

"I guess you thought wrong, pal." Dan unfolded his arms.

"Why don't you just butt out?"

Kate swallowed as the two men squared off at each other again, fists clenched. Rico's warning growl sounded a low, ominous tattoo, raising the hairs on her neck. Hastily, she moved between them.

"Charles, please, you'd better go. I'll . . . I'll call you tomorrow, at the hotel."

"Like hell you will!"

Kate blinked at Dan's snarl. Somehow, this business of being fought over by two attractive men wasn't living up to all her youthful romantic fantasies. It was unsettling. Downright uncomfortable, in fact. Kate's own temper began to rise. She took a firm grip on her composure, ignored Dan's thunderous scowl and hustled Charles out of the living room toward the front door.

"I'll call you," she told him, pushing him out into the night. With a sigh of relief, she leaned back against the door. Ruefully, she surveyed the ring of faces watching her with varying degrees of motherly glee, childish bewilderment and pure, unadulterated male possessiveness.

"We need to discuss your visitor," Dan growled, breaking the silence.

"I'd rather discuss your announcement," Kate told him sweetly.

"Me, too!" Mary Catherine added. Her wide grin turned to outright laughter as both Kate and Dan swung toward her. Consternation was plainly written on his face, an outright plea on hers. "But I guess I can wait until later to hear all the details. Come on, Jason. Let's wait for our pizza in the kitchen."

Kate waited until the kitchen door swung shut behind them before moving to the still, silent Dan. She stopped a few paces away, trying to read the expression in his glittering eyes. To her surprise, and relief, it was one of rueful laughter.

Dan reached out and pulled her into his arms. She felt an answering smile spread across her face as she leaned back in the strong circle of his embrace. Her breath caught as his hazel eyes turned smoky with desire and an indefinable emotion that made her heart thump painfully.

"I think someone mentioned something about marriage?" she prompted.

Dan grinned down at her. "Seems there are a number of men around here tonight with marriage on their minds. You want to fill me in on this Charles character?"

"Not really. He's history."

"He doesn't seem to realize that," Dan said dryly.

"Well, I was trying to make it clear when you, uh, flattened him."

Dan tightened his arms, narrowing the space between them. "I have this thing about seeing my woman in another man's arms. Old-fashioned, I admit, but now you know."

Kate slid her hands up his chest to curl them around his neck. Her hips settled intimately against the cradle of his thighs, discovering the rampant, insistent desire under the thin fabric of his cutoffs.

"Now I know," she whispered.

"What do you say we skip the pizza? I find I'm hungry for something else entirely."

* * *

"So when is the wedding? And where?" Mary Catherine perched on a rawhide stool and surveyed her daughter across the wide expanse of the kitchen counter. "Here, or in L.A.? Kathleen, are you listening to me?"

Kate looked up from the oranges she was feeding into the electric juicer. Noticing her mother's impatient glare, she turned the machine off. "Sorry, Mother, I didn't hear you."

"You've been off in la-la land since you got out of bed this morning! You promised a few details when you breezed out of here last night, young lady."

"We didn't quite get around to specifics," Kate told her with a sheepish grin.

"Well, of all the...!" Mary Catherine shook her head. "Don't you know you have to strike while the iron—not to mention the man—is hot?"

Kate burst out laughing at the total disgust on her mother's face. "I had enough trouble explaining Charles and soothing Dan's ruffled feathers to pin him down to the exact hour."

"Considering the fact that you didn't get back here until almost dawn, I think you could have settled the time, the place and the entire guest list," her mother rejoined tartly.

"We will," Kate promised.

"It's not like you have months to plan all this, you know." Mary Catherine's voice was almost grumpy. "Your lease is up in a couple of weeks, you've still got Jason to settle and you're spending every free moment lately on this darn marathon."

Kate sighed. "I know, I know. I've been thinking about Dan and me for weeks. Yet now that we've actually made the commitment, I can't seem to focus on details."

"And this is the woman who has her life all laid out in five-year increments! You better get with it, girl. The two of you have some major decisions to work out."

"The big decisions are the easiest," Kate said confidently, pouring them each a glass of juice.

"Oh? Like where you're going to live? And what you'll do about your business?"

"I can work out of Albuquerque as easily as L.A., so the business is no problem. And there are plenty of nice houses available here in this neighborhood. I called an agent on a couple of them."

"What does Dan say about your business?"

"We haven't actually discussed it, but he's supportive of my career goals."

Mary Catherine frowned. "A home and how you operate your business are major decisions, Kate. I think you and Dan should sit down and sort through them together."

"We will," she promised again, still too wrapped up in the delicious thought of marriage to Dan to worry about the details.

Her mother gave her daughter one last, exasperated look and climbed down off the stool. "You will let me know when you finally decide on a date, I hope!"

"You'll be the first, I promise." Kate laughed. "Now let's go get dressed and then unglue Jason from his keyboard. I promised to have us all down at the race center by noon to help with the last-minute registrations. Wear something comfortable."

The race headquarters was a scene of cheerful, controlled chaos on this day before the big event. Kate set

Jason and Mary Catherine to work sorting through the hundreds of last-minute applications. She herself joined a rank of volunteer hackers who were busily inputting data into the donated computers set up for the occasion. Eager participants and harried officials hustled around stacks of boxes, racks of bright vests to be worn by road guides and piles of T-shirts. The shirts came in every size from toddler to extra-extra large, and all proclaimed this year's Duke City Marathon the best yet.

Kate was showing a new volunteer how to use the scanner when Jason's caseworker called to ask if she could slip away for a few moments. Leaving Jason and Mary Catherine surrounded by a busy, laughing crowd of kids and indulgent parents, she headed downtown. During the short drive through the deserted streets, Kate was torn by conflicting emotions. She hoped that Mrs. Harris had found a good foster home for Jason, yet felt a confused reluctance to let him go. Somehow, the idea of sending Jason to someone else's home held less and less appeal.

"Thanks for coming in, Kate," the young woman greeted her. "I know you've been busy with the marathon, but we don't have much time left to work out a solution for Jason."

"No problem," Kate assured her, taking a seat in the small, neat office. In the weeks they'd worked together, Kate had grown to respect and admire Elizabeth Harris. A young mother and dedicated social worker, Liz put her heart and soul into her work. She took a personal interest in every one of her cases. She knew almost as well as Kate how Jason was doing in school, what his favorite computer game was and how his fears and insecurities had turned him into a quiet, contained, solemn youngster.

"I think I've found the perfect home." Liz pulled a thick folder toward her and opened it to scan an ink-filled form. "The Kents came down and applied for foster-parent status a few days ago. The psychological test results just came back, as well as the background checks. They're all good."

Liz sorted through the papers and pulled out the profile she'd compiled on the prospective foster parents. Most of the information was confidential, of course, but she could tell Kate enough to reassure her Jason would be going to a good home.

"The Kents are a middle-aged couple with three children of their own. Their youngest son just started high school and they want to share their home and their love with a child who needs help. I talked to all of their children. The boy in high school is outgoing and well adjusted, no reported problems of any kind. There's also a daughter at UNM and another married daughter in town with two children of her own. The whole family has a very positive focus. They're just the kind of family to give Jason the long-term stability he needs in these critical years."

Kate listened to Liz's account with a sinking feeling in her stomach. She'd wanted desperately to settle Jason in just such a stable environment. So why did the thought make her insides churn?

"I hate to spring this on you on such short notice, but would it be possible for Jason to meet with them this afternoon? I visited them yesterday and discussed his background. They're interested, but are leaving for a long-planned vacation on Sunday. If I'm going to wrap this up in the next couple weeks, I'll have to start the paperwork while they're gone."

Kate swallowed the lump in her throat. "Sure, we can make it. What time, and where?"

It was a quiet, subdued trio that met Dan for dinner at their favorite Mexican restaurant that evening.

"What's with everyone?" Dan asked, sliding into the booth beside Kate. "Why so glum? Did your computer program bomb and you lost a couple thousand marathoners?"

Kate mustered a thin smile and told him about the prospective foster home in a determined, cheerful voice. "The Kents are really nice, Dan. Mother and I only stayed for a few minutes of the interview, but we could see they liked Jason. They have a big home, so he would have a room of his own, and . . . and their son has a collection of computer games that made us both drool, right, Jason?"

The boy looked up from the soda he'd been stirring with a straw. The closed, sullen look that had almost disappeared from his eyes in the past few weeks was back. "Yeah, I guess so."

The meal passed uncomfortably. Kate tried to project a positive attitude, with Mary Catherine's help. Jason kept his eyes down. Dan observed them all calmly.

He slipped a hand around Kate's wrist when they drove up to her house, holding her in her seat. "We're going for a drive, Mary Catherine. We'll see you and Jason later."

"We won't wait up for you," Kate's knowing mother replied.

Kate didn't even try to make conversation as they drove through the deepening twilight. She hunched in her seat and nibbled at one fingernail nervously. Dan shot her an assessing look, but didn't say anything until they pulled into the parking lot of his apartment complex. He led her inside, then settled them both in one of the large leather sofas. His strong arms rested lightly on her waist and his broad shoulder was just the right height for her to lean her head against. Relaxing in his arms, she watched through the sliding glass doors as the flaming colors of sunset began to deepen far across the mesa.

"Okay, let's have it." His deep voice finally broke the stillness of the gathering night.

Kate sighed. "Oh, Dan, I can't believe how confused I am about all this. I thought I'd be so happy to find a family like the Kents for Jason, but..." Her voice trailed off. She didn't quite understand herself what the *but* meant.

"I tried to warn you not to get too close to him, honey."

"I know, I know. It's not that we're even that close, really. I mean, he rarely talks to me and we're not totally comfortable with each other all the time. Maybe it's just that I've gotten used to him," she said in a small voice.

Dan shifted her weight and pulled her closer. Kate could feel his warmth under her, infinitely soothing and reassuring.

"Don't sell yourself short. You've done a good job with the boy, and you're more than just 'used to' each other."

"It's just that we didn't have much time. I think I could have reached him, given a few more months." She watched the sun slip down behind Mount Taylor in a blaze of red and gold.

"I...I even thought about *us* adopting him," she said hesitantly, her eyes still on the far peak.

When Dan made no comment, she turned in his arms to face him. She could barely make out his features in the last, lingering light. "I've been thinking about it for days. I mean, we'll be living here. I'll move my business headquarters from L.A. We could get a house with room for Jason and Mary Catherine, when she wanted to visit."

Her voice picked up speed as the ideas which had been simmering in the back of her mind tumbled out. "There are a number of homes for sale up where I'm renting now. I went to look at one just a few streets down. It has lots of room for us and Jason—and even Rico. With an established home, we wouldn't have any trouble adopting Jason, or at least extending the custody arrangement. You've certainly got enough standing with Judge Chavez to swing it."

Her excitement faltered a bit at Dan's continuing silence. Realizing the whole scheme was a surprise to him, she rushed on. "It will work out fine. Honestly, Dan. Jason's a good kid, really. And I owe him. He's still not completely recovered psychologically from that beating. The visit to the Kents this afternoon upset him, I could see it. He needs—"

Kate broke off as Dan stood suddenly and set her on her feet. He walked across the room to turn on a lamp. The light cast a golden glow over the room. It also highlighted the stark, rigid planes of Dan's face.

"Is that why you're marrying me?" he asked, his voice low and taut.

"What?"

"To give Jason a home? To lift this guilt trip you've been on ever since he was hurt?"

Shocked, Kate gaped at him. "Dan, surely...you can't think I..." She stuttered in confusion. The fierce glare in his eyes deepened to a steady silvery flame.

"You've got it all worked out, haven't you? Kid, home, business. And a convenient marriage that ties it all together. Did you enter it all into your little computer and weigh the variables?"

"I thought you liked Jason," Kate got out, helpless in the face of his obvious anger.

"I do," he growled. "You know I do."

Kate felt her confusion growing to overwhelming proportions. "Then why does the idea of adopting him upset you so much? I know it's tough starting a marriage with a ready-made family, but lots of people do these days."

Dan strode forward, taking her arms in an iron grip. "Listen to me, Kate, and listen good. *Liking* is not a good enough reason to take a child into your home permanently. You have to take him into your heart. And *liking* sure as hell isn't a good enough reason to get married."

A searing shaft of hurt lanced through Kate. "What do you mean?" she whispered.

"I mean maybe we ought to think this through a little more. I love you, more than I'd ever dreamed it was possible to love anyone. But I'll be damned if I'm going to be just another neat phase in the new plans you've laid out for yourself. I want a say in decisions that affect our life, Kate. We'll shape our future together, or not at all."

Kate felt panic start to rise. "Dan, I'm sorry. I should have talked to you about these ideas and plans."

"You sure should have, lady. We should've talked about a lot of things." He gave an exasperated sigh and loosened his grip.

"It's just that there hasn't been any time!" Kate cried. "With this race hanging over us, and your responsibilities and mine, and—"

"I know, I know." Dan turned away and ran a hand through his hair. Kate watched, her heart in her throat. She couldn't be losing this man, she thought desperately. He'd become the center of her existence, the focal point of all her plans. Crossing the small space between them, she tugged gently on his arm.

"I love you, Daniel Kingman. With my whole heart and soul. I'm sorry if I've let my schemes and plans run away with me. They don't mean anything without you. Please, please, let me try again."

The last of the anger in Dan's eyes faded. He stared down at her for a long, quiet minute, then took her in his arms. He rested his chin on her head and they clung to each other in the stillness.

"Damn straight, we'll try again," he finally told her in a low, level voice. "I'm as much at fault as anyone in this. I haven't wanted to waste the few hours we've had alone together with talk. We haven't taken the time to sort things out in a measured way."

A surge of wild relief washed through Kate. Her arms tightened around his waist, and she nuzzled her cheek into the warm, scented hollow of his neck. The familiar tang of his after-shave and taste of his skin filled her, infinitely arousing and incredibly reassuring. Her arms slid up around his neck, pulling him even closer to her lips and darting tongue. Unconsciously, she rubbed her breasts against the hard planes of his chest.

His breath sounded harsh and ragged in her ear. "Dammit, Kate. That's what I mean! I can't think when you do that."

"That's the whole point, fella," she whispered.

Dan groaned and picked her up in his arms. "We *will* sit down and straighten out a few details of our lives . . . later."

They talked very little that night. In fact, Kate barely got home in time to wake Mary Catherine and Jason to get them ready for the start of the marathon.

Eleven

The day of the big race dawned bright and clear, with a cloudless blue sky and sharp-etched sunshine that only New Mexico could produce. A little before seven, Kate loaded Jason in running gear, Mary Catherine in a neon green volunteer T-shirt, and a grinning Rico with a rakish red handkerchief around his neck into the Audi.

Throughout the drive to the race center she tried to recapture the excitement she'd felt previously for the marathon. Still shaken from her near fight with Dan and confused about her reaction to the thought of Jason leaving, it was hard to do. The boy was as quiet as she was. Kate guessed he was thinking of the visit to the Kents, but by tacit agreement no one mentioned it.

The frenetic level of last-minute activity at the center soon caught them all up. They worked until nearly nine—even Rico, who provided impromptu baby-sitting services for the young children of several volunteers—

then joined the caravan of vehicles that made its way to
the finish line on Fourth Avenue. Kate had done all she
could with the prerace data entry. Now her assignment
was to oversee the ranks of volunteers at the finish point
who would input the times as the runners came across.
There were the three different race events to record: the
full twenty-six mile marathon, which Dan was partici-
pating in; a half marathon; and a five-kilometer fun run
that Jason entered.

They made their way from the underground parking
lot reserved for race officials and volunteers to the finish area. It was a scene of teeming color and noisy,
bustling activity. Police cars with flashing lights kept the
echoing downtown streets clear of traffic. Spectators
spread blankets and lawn chairs on sidewalks while race
officials and volunteers hurried back and forth setting
up relief stations. Street vendors were already hawking
everything from Sno-Kones to breakfast burritos. Kate
knew that the scene at the starting line some miles away
had to be just as chaotic, with the added presence of
more than three hundred runners warming up for the
full marathon. It would be even worse as thousands of
half marathoners converged later, and then the fun
runners.

A loudspeaker set on the roof of a TV van kept them
informed as the runners gathered at the starting line.
Kate cheered with everyone else when the sound of the
gunshot signaling the start boomed over the speakers,
then listened with half an ear to the race's progress. It
would be another three hours before the first runner
crossed the finish line, and she had plenty to keep her
occupied until then.

With Jason busy setting up tables and Mary Catherine helping out in the Gatorade brigade, Kate devoted

herself to organizing the bank of laptop computers that would record the events. She panicked momentarily when she discovered that the small, borrowed generator would provide only a three-hour supply of power. Luckily, half of the volunteers had brought back-up battery packs for their machines. Kate had a spare in the car, and she'd have to retrieve it as soon as there was a slack in the preparations.

The loudspeakers crackled as they blared out the news that the first runner passed the halfway point. The crowd at the finish line began to grow. One of the volunteer hackers crashed his hard disk and worked feverishly with Kate's determined assistance to get it back up. Even Jason helped, rerunning the operating software on Kate's machine to transfer to the reconstructed hard disk. While they were reloading the race program, they heard the excited announcer relate that a local favorite had taken the lead at the twenty-mile point. It wasn't Dan, but then he hadn't hoped to do more than finish respectably in this race. Tension began to grip the crowd as more and more people strained to see down the empty stretch. Tall buildings on either side of the city street echoed the almost palpable waves of excitement. Kate's own tension level peaked at about the same moment her computer screen flickered, then dimmed to an unreadable gray.

"Oh, no!"

"What?" Jason's blue eyes swung toward her.

"My battery's running down, and I forgot to get my back-up power pack from the car!"

"Can't you borrow one?"

"No, they're all in use," she groaned. "I can't believe it! After all the work we put into this blasted program, we won't even be able to help run it!"

"I'll go get the back-up," Jason volunteered.

"No, it'll take too long. You'll miss all the excitement. I'll go."

"The first runner's still a couple miles out. I can run to the car and be back before he crosses the line."

"Well . . ."

"I'll go, Kate. You'd never make it in time. You're, um, not exactly in shape, you know."

Kate's breath caught at the mischievous grin that spread across his face. It was so like the grin of a normal, happy eleven-year-old, and so unexpected on Jason's usually solemn face, that pain sliced through her. This was the way he should always look. This was the way she wanted him to look! Swallowing the sudden ache, she summoned up a cheeky, answering grin.

"I'm going to ignore that last remark," she replied, tossing him the keys to her car. "Move it, kid!"

When the first red lights of the advance convoy appeared, Jason still hadn't returned. The crowd surged to its feet. Far off in the distance came the muted roar of shouting and applause. Frowning, Kate scanned the edges of the band of volunteers. She spotted Mary Catherine and Rico and hurried over to them.

"Have you seen Jason? He went to get my power pack from the car and isn't back yet."

Her mother shook her head just as an armada of police cars, ambulances and TV vans turned onto Fourth and began heading toward them.

"Kate, they're coming!" One of the volunteers at the computer bank waved frantically.

Chewing on her lower lip, Kate ran back to the row of seated hackers. A quick glance told her they were as ready as they'd ever be to record the results. But even if they weren't, she couldn't worry about it now. Now she had to find Jason.

Asking her mother to tell Dan she'd gone looking for Jason, Kate edged her way out of the crowd and headed for the garage a few blocks away. Her sneakered feet slapped against the pavement, strangely loud in the deserted streets as she left the tumult of the race behind. Puffing, she ran down two flights of steps to the dim, subterranean level where she'd left her car.

The unease that had been curling in her belly with each step sharpened as her calls for Jason went unanswered in the cavernous depths. It turned to outright alarm when she dashed around the end of the row where her car was parked. The Audi's trunk gaped open and her power pack lay on the concrete a few feet away.

"Jason! Jason, where are you?"

Fighting down a swamping fear, she scooped up the power pack by its strap and slammed down the trunk. For an endless moment she stood leaning on the fender, her blood hammering in her ears, her throat constricted.

She shouted for him again, panic adding a hint of shrillness to her voice.

"Kate!"

The thin, muffled cry was cut off almost immediately, but it was enough to send Kate running for the far end of the garage. She rounded a pickup truck and skidded to a halt, her eyes searching the dim area frantically. At the sound of a thud and a keening cry her head whipped around. To her right, in the dark shadows of a corner stall, two figures bent over Jason. One figure drew his foot back even as she watched and swung it toward the boy in a vicious arc.

Without stopping to think, Kate yelled at the top of her lungs and ran toward them. She swung the only weapon she had in a wild loop over her head. The power pack only weighed about six pounds, but it was better than nothing.

Both men turned in startled surprise at her ferocious charge. The one closest to Kate flung up an arm as she brought the power pack down at his head with all her strength. It hit his forearm with a solid thud. The rifle crack of splitting bone sounded a second before his scream of pain. He doubled over and sank to his knees, his arm cradled against his chest.

"Hey!" The second man jumped back, out of the circle of the whirling pack.

Wild anger made Kate reckless. She stepped over Jason's still-prone body and swung again.

"Kate, no!"

"You stupid bitch."

Jason's cry and the man's shouted curse rang in her ears. The man—no, Kate could see now he wasn't a man, but a lean, wiry teenager—ducked. And came up with a long, vicious-looking knife in his hand.

Kate dragged air and fear in equal parts into her lungs. She backed away from the gleaming blade, stooping to haul Jason up and into her arms.

"Stay right where you are, lady. I ain't never used this knife on a woman before, but I got a real urge to right now."

Half crouching, he edged around her to his fallen comrade. Kate's fear turned to sick dread as she saw the sweat glistening on his face and the nervous way he tossed the knife from hand to hand. Under his thin T-shirt, his stomach muscles twitched uncontrollably. She'd never seen a drug user before, but it was obvious

this kid was high on something and she didn't think it
had anything to do with the excitement from the race.

"Danny! Danny, you okay?"

"She broke my arm," the other boy moaned, rolling
on the floor in pain.

The teen holding the knife turned back to her, his face
twisted in an ugly sneer.

"You're gonna pay for that, bitch."

"No, Pete, leave her alone!"

Kate stared down, astounded, as Jason pushed himself out of her arms and took two shaky steps toward
the other boy.

"Jason, do you know these guys? Are they your...
your gang?"

The older boy laughed, and the sound sent goose
bumps shivering down Kate's arms.

Jason sent her a wide, scared look over his shoulder.
"No, Kate..." he started.

"You sniveling little wimp," the older boy spat. "You
were happy enough to be part of my gang before."

"I wasn't, Pete! I never wanted to be part of this."

"Is that why you turned us in to the cops? Your own
damn brother?"

"No! No! I didn't!"

Neither of them appeared to hear Kate's swift, in-
drawn breath. They formed a macabre tableau in the
dim light: a menacing, crouching figure with an obscene knife in his hands; a thin, frightened boy in white
running shorts; and Kate, the power pack still dangling
from her fingers.

"The police have been harassing our gang for weeks,
ever since you went to live with this broad. I done some
checking, Jase. She's shacking up with a cop and you're
in with them, right in the middle."

"No, I never said anything, Pete. Honest!"

"I thought the beating we gave you would teach you something. Instead you sicced the cops on us. You need another lesson, Jase. Her, too!"

The knife flashed as he swung it in a wide arc, moving toward them slowly on the balls of his feet. Kate's fingers tightened on the strap, and she pushed Jason behind her.

"Leave him alone," she ground out. "He never said a word about any of you. Believe me, I would've remembered if Jason happened to mention that it was his own brother who sent him to the hospital."

The vitriolic scorn in her voice stopped him. For a breathless moment, Kate thought she might have shamed him into letting them go. But then the other boy groaned, a long, ragged sob of pain that sliced through the still air.

Pete stiffened, and his eyes took on a wild, feral glaze that told Kate he was going to lunge.

She shoved Jason away from her and swung the pack.

"Run, Jason!" she screamed.

"No, Pete!"

"Get back, Kate!"

Dan's frantic shout crashed into her consciousness at the same instant a savage growl sounded right behind her left ear. She whirled and took a glancing blow from a flying black body as it sailed through the air and landed with a slam against Pete's chest. Fear ripped through her, until she saw the hand gripping the knife caught in Rico's snarling mouth.

Heavy footfalls pounded the concrete behind her.

"Hold him, Rico," Dan shouted.

Rico was more than happy to oblige. The knife clattered to the pavement, and the screaming boy went down under the onslaught of a hundred pounds of snarling, twisting beast.

"Are you okay? Kate! Jason! Are you okay?"

Other footsteps sounded as a couple of uniformed officers ran up, but Kate barely noticed them. She and Jason were wrapped in Dan's hard, sweat-slicked embrace. His arm crushed her ribs, the pin holding the race number to his tank top bit into her cheek, and Kate had never felt anything so wonderful in her entire life.

By the time the last of the squad cars drove away and Dan had bundled Kate and her family into the Audi, she'd almost stopped shaking. And by the time they pulled into her garage and piled out of the car, she was able to make her own, if unsteady, way into the house.

While Mary Catherine and Dan went into the kitchen to get them all much-needed sustenance, she sank down on the couch and let the last of the fear drain from her body.

"Thanks, Kate."

Jason's thin, hesitant form hovered beside the couch, his face pale and his blue eyes staring from a face that looked much too old for a child. Kate's throat tightened once more, this time with a need to cry so sharp, it took every ounce of her depleted strength to hold it back. She lifted trembling hands to the boy.

With a muffled sob, he flung himself into her arms. Her own tears began to flow, washing runnels down her cheeks as she clutched his body to hers. They rocked against each other, bonded by shared fear, by relief and by something else, something Kate struggled to understand. When Jason finally lifted his head, she met his tear-washed look with one of her own. At that moment, she knew what that other something was.

* * *

"I love him, Dan."

Her low voice was barely audible above the bubbling of the hot tub. It was late, well after midnight. An exhausted Jason had finally fallen into bed, Mary Catherine was sound asleep and even Rico was absent from his usual post beside them. Sated from the feast of steak and chili Mary Catherine had fed him in honor of his hero status, the dog slept blissfully beside Jason's bed. Only Dan and Kate were awake, and she'd managed at last to coax him into the hot tub to soak away the residue of tension.

Dan leaned against one of the backrests, his legs splayed out in front of him. Kate lay with her back against his chest, her arms resting on the forearms wrapped around her waist, her head lolling comfortably on his shoulder. A bright, full moon hung over the mountains and bathed the deck, making it seem as if they floated in a pool of liquid, bubbling silver.

"When his own brother pulled that knife on us today, my heart stopped. I would have strangled the bastard with my bare hands before I let him hurt Jason again."

She floated against Dan, feeling the smooth satin of his skin beneath her bare thighs and buttocks. "He's been hurt so much already, Dan. I knew then that if... when... we got away, I couldn't let him go."

Holding her breath, Kate waited for him to say something. Bubbles broke against the water's surface in an iridescent foam. Far off in the distance, a lone coyote called to its mate. Finally, after what seemed like an eternity, Dan shifted slightly on his seat and turned her in his arms. The hazy silver of his eyes gleamed richer and more luminous than moonlight on the water.

"So we won't let him go," he said.

Kate searched his eyes. "Do you really mean it? I know you had doubts about taking Jason in. Are you sure you—"

"I never had any doubts about Jason," he interrupted gently. "But I had doubts about why you wanted him. Guilt is no substitute for love. I learned a long time ago you can't force that love."

"Oh, Dan . . ."

His lips cut off her tremulous cry. Kate flung her arms around his neck and slithered her wet body up his until she returned his kiss with all her pent-up emotion.

"Good Lord." Dan's chest heaved under her when he broke off contact some moments later. "If this damn contraption wasn't already heating me past the safe point, that kiss would have done it! No, wait!"

He took her hips in a firm hold and pushed her back down his long, wet torso. Anchoring her legs with one of his, Dan held her immobile.

"Wait a minute, Kate, before I disintegrate on the spot." He dragged in several deep breaths, which he realized instantly was a mistake. His chest hair tickled Kate's already-aroused nipples and turned them into hard, aching buds.

"Sorry, Captain Kingman. I'm afraid I can't wait," she breathed, while her hands and her mouth and her hips went to work.

Just before the stars exploded all around him, Dan admitted that maybe there was something to this hot tub business after all.

Epilogue

Kate thought her heart would burst with pride as she waited to walk through the rows of guests toward the two figures waiting for her in the gazebo. They stood side by side in matching gray cutaways, one tall, dark and indescribably handsome, the other small, sandy-haired and beaming with excitement. Rich organ music filled the square, rolling off the surrounding adobe buildings in sonorous waves.

A light breeze lifted her short veil, giving her a clearer picture of the colorful crowd filling the square. Half the guests wore police uniforms, the other half sported everything from dark jeans and cowboy hats to bright silks and flowered dresses. Kate was amazed at the number of guests. With less than a week to arrange everything, she hadn't expected this big a turnout. Both she and Mary Catherine had protested the short notice during a lively dinner discussion the day after the marathon.

Dan had told them calmly he wasn't going to take a chance on any more stray fiancés or lost brothers showing up. He wanted the thing sewed up as soon as possible. He'd already asked Judge Chavez to perform the ceremony the following Saturday in the plaza of Old Town. Kate couldn't have come up with a more romantic setting for a wedding. Her objections melted away.

With the enthusiastic help of Trish and Mary Catherine's bingo buddies, Kate had managed to pull it off. Invitations were printed and distributed within two days. Dan took charge of outfitting himself and Jason. Trish arranged the reception, then accompanied Kate and Mary Catherine on a wild shopping expedition.

The shopping trip was extravagantly successful. Kate found a lustrous satin gown studded with seed pearls along its low, rounded neckline and bell-shaped short sleeves. It hugged her long body to the hips, then fell in swirling folds of glistening white to the floor. A short train swept behind her as she walked. The gown's stunning simplicity was in inverse proportion to its cost, but Kate knew every penny was well spent when she started down the aisle on Dr. Chavez's arm.

Dan came down the few steps in front of the gazebo to take her hand. Her gaze fastened on his magnificent figure and smiling eyes. He stood with one foot resting on the first step, his outstretched hand holding hers. The arch above him trailed garlands of white roses, baby's breath and fluttering white satin ribbons. Against the white background, his dark hair and rakish mustache caught both her breath and her eyes.

She smiled, radiant with love and joy. Dan's hand tightened around hers and one corner of his mouth lifted in a lopsided grin that made her heart ache. Together, they ascended the few steps to where Trish, Jason and a beaming Judge Chavez waited for them.

"You're a beautiful bride, Mrs. Kingman."

Dan's deep, dark voice shivered across her senses. Kate stirred sleepily. When his hand slid under the light covering to stroke her breast, she moaned.

"Is that passion or sleep?"

"Both," she groaned, rolling over onto her back.

Dan leaned on one elbow, head in his hand, looking down at her. In the dim light of the one candle still fluttering in its crystal holder, Kate saw desire flowing in his eyes like molten silver. His free hand rested lightly on her breast, the fingers just brushing against its tip.

As if it had a will of its own, her own hand slipped out from under the covers to slide along his chest. Dark, curly hair trapped her fingers. Beneath them, his heart beat an increasingly erratic rhythm.

"I don't know if I have the energy left for this," she said, half laughing, half serious.

"What?" He scowled down at her ferociously. "Already reneging on your vows to love and cherish?"

"I've cherished you twice tonight. If you want this marriage to last longer than twenty-four hours, you'll have to let me recharge my batteries."

Her batteries started recharging on their own when his hand left her breast to trail down across the soft flesh of her belly. His callused fingers rasped against her skin, raising delightful shivers from her neck to her knees. She nearly moaned again when they buried themselves in the tangled curls between her legs. Her head fell back on the pillow in lazy passion. Her breath came in shallow gasps.

To her surprise, his fingers ceased their magic and Dan rolled out of bed. Kate propped herself up on both elbows to watch him stroll across the room. Utterly confused, she waited while he rooted through the small gym bag he'd brought with him on their weekend honeymoon. She'd teased him about bringing so little, only to be reminded that honeymooners didn't need any clothes anyway.

"Here." He tossed a little package onto the bed. "I was going to save this for our fiftieth anniversary, when we're old and gray and need something to stimulate our senses. But I think I'll make it a wedding present, instead."

"What is this?" Kate eyed the plain, brown paper wrapping dubiously. She wasn't the kind for kinky sex aids, and didn't think Dan was, either.

"Open it."

Kate chewed at one corner of her lower lip.

"Trust me, Katey mine. It's art. Beautiful, sensuous, wonderful art." His laughing eyes encouraged her.

Frowning, she slid a finger under the edge of the wrapping. The brown paper fell away, leaving a plain, unmarked videocassette in her hand. She gave him a puzzled, questioning look.

He took the cassette and slipped it into the VCR. Their luxurious suite came equipped with TVs and every other modern amenity in each of its four rooms.

Nervously, Kate watched gray lines flash across the screen in dizzying horizontal patterns. Gradually, they settled, then cleared entirely. Kate gasped as the familiar dimensions of her bedroom slowly took on definition. The camera swept the room once, twice, then came back to the open sliding glass doors just beyond her bed. As if an unseen hand were operating a zoom lens,

the area beyond the doors grew. Dark patterns resolved into separate, distinct shapes. The eye of the
camera adjusted, and one of the objects became a round
hot tub! Clearly visible above the rim of the tub was a
profile of her head, shoulders and the swell of her
breasts.

"Dan Kingman! I don't believe you had the nerve to
bring this on our honeymoon." Kate's voice sputtered
with choked laughter. She tore her embarrassed gaze
from the flickering screen to find her husband grinning
down at her.

"I never go anywhere without it," he told her sim-
ply.

Embarrassed, exasperated, enthralled, Kate pulled
him down beside her. The tape ran on, then ran out.
Flickering shadows danced over the two oblivious figures on the wide, rumpled bed.

Dan arched above Kate, his powerful body poised.
She lay panting under him, her arms wrapped tight
around the strong column of his neck.

"The real thing is so much better than the tape," Dan
murmured, before he lost the power of speech altogether.

* * * * *

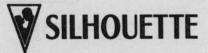

Cruel Legacy

One man's untimely death deprives a wife of her husband, robs a man of his job and offers someone else the chance of a lifetime...

Suicide — the only way out for Andrew Ryecart, facing crippling debt. An end to his troubles, but for those he leaves behind the problems are just beginning, as the repercussions of this most desperate of acts reach out and touch the lives of six different people — changing them forever.

Special large-format paperback edition

**OCTOBER
£8.99**

W●RLDWIDE

SILHOUETTE
Desire

COMING NEXT MONTH

FAMILY FEUD
Barbara Boswell

Man of the Month

Shelby thought her blue blood couldn't mix with Garrett's blue-collar background. But Garrett vowed that before long he'd be teaching her about mergers and acquisitions…of the most intimate kind!

THE UNFORGIVING BRIDE
Joan Johnston

Children of Hawk's Way

Falcon Whitelaw had vowed never to get married. So why was he saying 'I do' to widowed mother Mara—a woman who hated his guts?

LEMON
Lass Small

Brown Brothers

Lemon Covington hated fortune-hunting females who wanted big rings on their fingers. Then he met Renata—but she wouldn't bother to notice him. So what could this confirmed bachelor do?

SILHOUETTE

Desire

COMING NEXT MONTH

MEGAN'S MIRACLE
Karen Leabo

Megan was flabbergasted when Holt Ramsey claimed she was the natural mother of his adopted son! But why was there something hauntingly familiar about the boy?

OUTBACK NIGHTS
Emilie Richards

Russet Ames thought she was on her way to a new life in Australia. But she hadn't counted on old family friend Daniel Marlin meeting her at the airport…

UNDER THE BOARDWALK
Carla Cassidy

Greyson Blakemore was back—and he wouldn't let Nikki forget about the fiery kisses they'd once shared. But Nikki had vowed never to let him back into her life…

COMING NEXT MONTH FROM

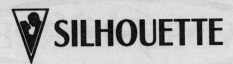 SILHOUETTE

Sensation

A thrilling mix of passion, adventure and drama

SECRET FIRES Kristin James
COLD, COLD HEART Ann Williams
KIDNAPPED! Kate Carlton
WICKED SECRETS Justine Davis

Intrigue

Danger, deception and desire— new from Silhouette...

SQUARING ACCOUNTS Patricia Rosemoor
CUTTING EDGE Caroline Burnes
DÉJÀ VU Laura Pender
CACHE POOR Margaret St. George

Special Edition

Satisfying romances packed with emotion

THE PARSON'S WAITING Sherryl Woods
A HOME FOR THE HUNTER Christine Rimmer
RANCHER'S HEAVEN Robin Elliott
A RIVER TO CROSS Laurie Paige
MIRACLE CHILD Kayla Daniels
FAMILY CONNECTIONS Judith Yates

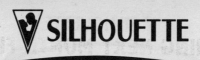

SILHOUETTE

WORDSEARCH

Win a year's supply of Silhouette Special Editions
ABSOLUTELY FREE!

Yes, you can win a whole year's supply of Silhouette Special Editions. It's easy, just find the hidden words in the grid below!

SPECIAL

MYSTERY

EDITION

TEDDY

SILHOUETTE

GIFT

S	L	O	V	E	A	Z	H	G	S
G	I	E	D	I	T	I	O	N	U
O	I	L	W	B	O	O	K	T	E
O	S	F	H	C	P	S	I	E	C
D	P	L	T	O	W	F	S	D	N
K	E	G	R	X	U	R	S	D	A
I	C	M	Y	S	T	E	R	Y	M
Z	I	A	N	A	R	D	T	K	O
T	A	N	Q	U	I	D	I	T	R
P	L	E	B	J	M	Y	L	S	E

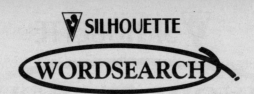

SILHOUETTE

WORDSEARCH

The first five correct entries out of the bag after the closing date will win one year's supply of Silhouette Special Editions (six books every month for twelve months). Worth over £100! **What could be easier?**

Don't forget to enter your name and address in the space below then put this page in an envelope and post it today (you don't need a stamp). Competition closes 30th June 1995.

SILHOUETTE WORDSEARCH
HARLEQUIN MILLS & BOON,
FREEPOST,
PO BOX 344,
CROYDON CR9 9EL.

COMP195

Are you a Reader Service subscriber   Yes ☐   No ☐

Ms/Mrs/Miss/Mr _____

Address _____

_____

_____ Postcode _____